THE HOBBYSHOP BOYS

✩ ✩ ✩

A Story of Technical Agents
In The Air Force Office Of
Special Investigations

JACK D. DYER

ISBN: 1499295626
ISBN 13: **9781499295627**
Library of Congress Control Number: **2014908202**
CreateSpace Independent Pub. Platform
North Charleston, South Carolina

I dedicate this book to all of the men and women, past and present, who served and are serving their country in the Technical Services Division of the Air Force Office of Special Investigations (OSI) and especially to my Division Chief, good friend and hunting buddy, Dave Gabourie.

ACKNOWLEDGEMENTS

I wish to thank my wonderful wife, Michele, for always being there for me for the past fifty-one years and for supporting my efforts with this book by being both a critic and reviewer. To our children, Tad, Heather and Shaun for putting up with all of those moves around the world, being in some difficult situations and enjoying all of those good times together.

I also wish to thank all of the great people in OSI who provided me with support and encouragement, who mentored me through all of the training and experiences that were required to become a Technical Services Special Agent and who over the years have remained friends that I truly appreciate.

I want to thank my friend, Jan Elliott, for giving me the inspiration to start this project and for introducing me to the guys and gals at the Fort Collins Pen Pointers in Fort Collins, Colorado who helped me with this project initially. I also want to thank Bob Doerr, Jim Huckabee, Ray Lyon, Jack Matthews, Jim Deitz, Penny Lloyd, Dave Gabourie, Ray Spangler, Carolynn Smith and my very good friend Richard K. for helping me with my manuscript. I also want to thank Molly Lovas for the expert guidance with my manuscript and her patience with such a novice as I.

FORWARD

The Hobbyshop Boys follows the career of the fictitious Jake Douglas in the Technical Services Division (TSD) of the Air Force Office of Special Investigations (OSI). The TSD is one of the elite portions of OSI. In the late 1960's and 1970's, OSI had approximately fifteen hundred special agents but only one hundred and fifty special agents in TSD. This story begins with Jake's selection process for entry into OSI. It proceeds through the intensive Special Investigators' Course that all OSI agents had to attend, through the special training required for technical agents and, finally, through some of his early technical support operations.

CONTENTS

OPERATION II: THE DRUG RUNNERS

OPERATION III

OPERATION IV

OPERATION V: THEFT OF CLOTHING ITEMS

PART I

SPECIAL INVESTIGATORS' COURSE

USAF Special Investigators School (OSI)
Location: Washington, D.C.

CHAPTER 1

The sun had just risen over the tops of the drab, gray buildings that lined the narrow street on the north end of Bolling Air Force Base (BAFB) in Southwest Washington, D.C. I was completing my morning jog and heading back to the old enlisted personnel military barracks where I had spent the previous night.

Military Barracks on BAFB Photo by SA Roche

My blue sweats, covering my five foot ten inch frame, were discolored with perspiration. My name is Jake Douglas. I had been up since 5:00 am and would put in about forty-five minutes of exercise and then take a hot shower. That would give me time to get some breakfast and coffee at the chow hall. I had to be ready to catch the bus at 7:40 am for the trip into Washington, D.C. and my new class that I am here to attend.

Today is Monday, April 21, 1969. I am twenty-eight years old. It is the first day of the Special Investigators' Course I will be attending, now that I have recently been accepted by OSI. It had been a long process to be accepted as a technical agent for OSI.

After returning to the U.S. from a three-year assignment in West Germany in 1967, I was assigned to work in the Communications Squadron at Selfridge Air Force Base near Mt. Clemens, Michigan.

I had no idea where that was at first. I soon found out it was just a few miles north of Detroit. The one lasting memory about my time in Michigan was that I had met a guy named Monty Jones. He and his family lived on a farm near Shelby, MI where I worked part time at a service station to supplement my Air Force income.

Monty worked at the station with me, and we became good friends. Monty invited me out to his farm and taught me how to hunt pheasants. He also had a cabin near Gaylord, MI, which was in the northern portion of the state. We would go up there sometimes in the winter and hunt deer and ice fish. It was a great escape from my duties at Selfridge AFB.

Working in ground radio maintenance in Germany had not been bad, because of the variety of equipment I had been able to work on. The location where I worked, outside of Ramstein Air Base, had been a WWII German military command center bunker in an underground cave complex near Kindsbach, Germany. Germany had been a great place to be in the mid-1960's. The German Mark was still at the good exchange rate of four marks for one U.S. dollar so the living was good. In addition, the German food and beer – well, it was wunderbar! I was able to travel around

Germany and really enjoyed the country and the people. One of the best places I went to was Bad Durkheim for the "Wine Fest," which is the largest wine festival in the world. It was held in the fall, after the harvest, and the Germans played just as hard as they worked. The Wine Fest was held in huge tents that were approximately fifty yards long, and filled with tables and benches. There was always the German Band in their Lederhosen shorts with leather suspenders. The entire purpose of the Wine Fest, I believe, was to see who could get the drunkest – drinking wine in half-liter glasses – and still walk.

People would sit on the benches, sway back and forth with the music, sing and, of course, drink lots of wine!

However, after being stationed for a year at Selfridge working on the same boring type of radio equipment, I realized I just really did not like working in radio maintenance. Therefore, I started taking an evening college class in accounting in the fall of 1968. Looking back, I am not sure now exactly what I thought I was going to do with a college degree, if I ever got one, but it was something that held the promise of a way to get out of radio. While taking that evening class, I met two OSI special agents who were in the class and stumbled upon my possible way out of radio! As we began to talk during class breaks, they became very interested in me when they found out I was working in ground radio maintenance. As it turns out, at that time, OSI had begun a serious recruitment program for technical agents and had put out the word to all OSI Offices to look for personnel to recruit.

They were specifically interested in personnel currently working in radio maintenance because of their schooling and training in radio theory and electronics maintenance.

Since I had held a security clearance for several years and was working in radio maintenance, I expected the recruitment and acceptance process with OSI to be short. However, that had not been the case at all. It was now April 1969, and I had submitted my application in October of the previous year. No one would tell me why the process had taken so long, but it really did not matter.

All that mattered now was I would start training and soon be a special agent in OSI. Therefore, the bottom line at that time was that it was not as important that I was getting into OSI as I was getting out of radio! Of course, another big advantage of being in OSI, compared to radio maintenance, was I would get to wear civilian clothes daily instead of my Air Force Uniforms. However, in truth, it was a major move in my life. It was one I enjoyed more than any other job I have ever had, and it opened many doors for me later in life.

I had arrived at BAFB Sunday morning after flying from Detroit, MI to Washington National Airport. After arriving at BAFB, I was directed to the old military barracks that were used to house the OSI students who were attending the Special Investigators School. Upon entering the barracks, I met the class leader for the next student class, Technical Sergeant Frank Kurgland. As a technical sergeant, Frank was the ranking enlisted man in the new class, and as such with normal military tradition, had been picked to be the barracks leader. I was a staff sergeant, as were most of the other men in the class, except for the few officers. Frank was a stout man, about six feet tall, kind of round faced and one who had a pleasant smile. He was very easy to get to know and seemed to like everyone. Little was I to know at that time, I would work for him later in the civilian world.

"What is your job going to be in OSI, if you make it through the school?" Frank asked.

"I'm going to be a technical agent when I graduate from the school," I replied.

"Kind of sure about yourself, aren't you?"

"That's the only way I know how to be."

"That's what I like about us technical types; we grab the bull by the horns!"

"So, you're going to be a technical agent also? What career field were you in?" I asked.

"Radio maintenance and I still am. They'll be keeping us in that career field from what I hear."

"Yes, that's what I heard also."

"I've already had one other technical type check in. Do you want to room with him?" Frank asked.

"I might as well. We need to stick together as I'm sure we will be outnumbered by the regular agents from what I'm told."

"I think you're correct; however, I've been informed there will be six potential technical agents in this class."

"Wow, I didn't expect that. In fact, I thought I might be the only one. That's great."

Frank assigned me to one of the two man rooms and told me my roommate was probably there. Upon arriving at the room to which I had been assigned, I saw what appeared to be a "man-mountain" lying on a bed. I entered the room and threw my suitcase down on the other empty bed.

I could not help but notice that the other man had taken the bed I would have chosen had I gotten there first.

Man-mountain got up and stuck out his huge hand. "Hello," he said in a deep, southern drawl. "My name's George Carriby."

"I'm Jake Douglas. I take it from your drawl that you must be from New England," I said with a smirk on my face.

"That would be taking it wrong," he answered in a long slow voice with an equally sly grin. "Actually, I'm from down near Austin, Texas."

"Well, you certainly had me fooled," I replied with an air of jest. "I am just kidding, of course. I hail from just a little north of Texas, from a place called Tulsa, Oklahoma."

"Ah, so you're an Okie, huh? I've known quite a few Okies; some of them aren't too bad."

"Do you like country music?" George asked.

"For the most part, with a little rock-n-roll thrown in," I stated.

"Well, I don't know so much about that rock-n-roll, although some of it ain't too bad. But, as long as you like country, we should get along jus' fine."

"I understand from Frank Kurgland that you're going to be a technical agent," I said.

"Yep, that's right. Are you?"

"Yes, I was in radio maintenance. Is that what you worked in?"

"Yep, as far as I know that's all they recruit from," replied George.

"I'm so glad to be out of that field. Are there any more of us technical types here?"

"I haven't met any yet, but I understand there'll be several of us," he said.

"So, how long have you been in the Air Force?" I asked

"Going on ten years, jus' about. If this job works out, I guess that I'll stay in for twenty," George replied. "How about you?"

"Well I have about nine years in right now. I got out after my first four years and was out for a little over a year. That was in 1964. While I was out, I joined an Air Force Reserve outfit and was promoted to staff sergeant. Then, when McNamara closed down, many of the reserve outfits in mid-1964, I was given an opportunity to go back into the active Air Force and go to Germany, so I decided to do that. Turns out, that was one of my best decisions. I plan to stay in for twenty and then retire."

"So, what'd you do before you came into the Air Force?" I asked.

"I was just a normal Texas ranch kid, nothing special. I finished school and worked on the family ranch. I eventually got hitched to my high school sweetheart named Molly. After a couple of years, we had a son and named him George, Jr. We continued to live and work on the ranch. I finally got purdy tired of that life and had some younger brothers to help Dad, so I decided to go into the military. I have found a home, I guess, and just hope that I can pass this training and like the job. Molly and Jr. both like to travel and see new places."

"How about you? What'd you do before the military?" George asked.

"Oh, I was like you in a way. I just barely managed to squeak through high school. I grew up in a broken home, and Mom had gotten married a couple of times after my dad. From about the eighth grade on, it had just been Mom and four kids. I was the oldest, so I had to help around the house a lot and watch the others. When we moved to Ventura, California, I was in the eleventh grade. I met a guy who was one year ahead of me, and we became good friends. His name was Jerry Benson. It was not until later in life I realized he became more of an older brother figure to me than anything else. He taught me how to fish for trout and to fish off the pier in Ventura. Anyway, he finished high school in 1958, the year before me, and just hung around waiting for me to graduate so we could join the Air Force together. Well, in about May of 1959, the darned Air Force Recruiter finally convinced Jerry he really needed to join the Air Force that month, so he did. We agreed I would join in June after school was out, and we would see each other at Lackland Air Force Base in Texas. So, Jerry left, I joined the Air Force in June and never saw him again until four or five years later."

"Darn, that's quite a story!"

"Yeah, shit happens as they say. Anyway, I guess I was made for the military, as I've really enjoyed it so far."

George and I hit it off right away since we were both country guys and, therefore, a little different than most of the others in class who were city folk. He was a big man, but was really a gentle giant. I guessed him to be about twenty-eight years old. We spent the rest of the day getting to know each other, meeting some other people who were arriving and preparing for our new life to start on Monday.

So, at 7:40 am, Monday morning, we piled into the Air Force bus for the ride from BAFB to Washington, D.C. Some of the group had met over the previous weekend and had already introduced themselves. Some people had continued to arrive on Sunday. I obviously had missed the arrival of at least one person – the one person I had hoped never to see again. And there he was getting on the bus, Skip Felton, my least favorite person in the world. We glared at each other, but did not say a word. He sat down as far away from me as he could get. We had a long history of personal conflict going back to our electronic maintenance schooling at Keesler Air

Force Base, in Biloxi, MS. We had been together on three different assignments and were friends at first. Skip was one of those people who gave a false first impression. People would be better off if they just chose to leave him alone. Skip was out for Skip, and that was the only way to put it. Once he had figured a person out, he would scheme about how to use them in any way he could.

I had paid the price, and it had been a dear one. During our second assignment together, I had given him some insight on how to improve a work method we were using. He had submitted the idea as his own. Not only did he get credit for the new work method and increased job performance, but also he received a substantial monetary reward and got a promotion in rank. He also used several other people in our organization in a like manner and, because of his promotion, ended up in charge of me and many other people. I always figured he would get his just reward someday, and maybe I could be instrumental in that demise now that we were going to be in the same outfit again.

As the bus departed BAFB, there was a high level of excitement in the air and, of course, a lot of chatter among everyone on the bus. This was a big day for all of us. It was a turning point in most of our lives. Although not many had talked about it yet, we were all in the same situation. We were getting out of a job we no longer wanted to do and hopefully getting into something brand new and exciting. As we neared D.C. and started seeing some of the larger national landmarks and historical buildings, the chatter got louder. It was amazing for the majority of us who had never been to D.C. to start seeing the monuments and expansive buildings. The National Mall itself was quite a sight to see, as it was a grassy expanse, two to three blocks wide, and it stretched in both directions from where we entered it for what seemed to be a very long distance.

Someone hollered, "Look there's the Washington Monument." At about the same time, someone else yelled, "Look there is the Smithsonian Museum Buildings." Finally, someone stated, "Look there's the National Capitol Building right in front of us." We were delivered to the World War I "Tempo E Building" which was located between Fifth and Seventh Streets, right on the National Mall. We were to find out later that the Tempo E Building was one of the last of the temporary office buildings that had been created to fulfill the need for office space in Washington, D.C. during the First World War. With the exterior of the building having been made out of concrete, the Tempo Buildings had lasted a lot longer than they were intended to. The last two Tempo Buildings had finally been torn down in 1970.

As we arrived, I thought to myself, *damn, this certainly is an old run down looking building. Couldn't OSI do better than this for their headquarters? Why is it located right on the National Mall in D.C.?*

Detail of Birdseye view from 1940's, shows the World War I Tempo E building remaining on the Mall between Fifth and Seventh Streets, above center of photo. Courtesy of National Park Service, National Mall and Memorial Parks

CHAPTER 2

After arriving at Tempo E, we were given directions, and told to proceed to the cafeteria. We were to wait there for someone to take us to our classroom. Upon entering the cafeteria, I selected an empty table, located in one of the rear corners of the room, and George and I sat down there. It was a habit of mine. I felt the overwhelming need to have my back to a wall and to be able to see everyone coming and going in a room.

After sitting down, I observed that, in addition to our new group, there were many other people sitting in the cafeteria. With the plain white walls and shiny steel fixtures, it gave the appearance of a rather sterile environment.

Our group was dressed in our Air Force Khaki, Class B Uniforms, and I saw that most of the other people in the room were in the same uniforms.

I assessed each person in the room, which was another habit of mine. I could see most of our group looked nervous and somewhat out of place. There were also quite a few people, dressed as we were, but much more relaxed and sitting in groups. We were to find out later those people were in the class ahead of us, with the exception of four people dressed in civilian suits, huddled together in the opposite corner of the room. They appeared to be checking out the nervous individuals.

Suddenly, a shapely, blonde woman, who looked to be in her early thirties, entered the room. What small amount of chatter that had been present in the room came to an abrupt halt. The four "suits" who had been sitting huddled together immediately got up and started out of the room.

The woman looked around the room and, in a calm voice stated, "All of those people who are here for the Special Investigators' Course that begins today, please follow me." As George and I stood up, I saw that all the rest of the nervous people stood up and followed the woman.

As the group was walking down a narrow, dingy hallway, George had gotten in front of me, and I noticed for the first time just how much larger than most of the other people he was. He certainly stood out in a crowd. I guessed him at about six feet three inches tall and in the neighborhood of three hundred pounds. He could very easily have passed as a lineman for the Washington Redskins.

I glanced around to see where Felton had gotten away to and saw he was walking behind me towards the rear of the pack. He was talking to another one of the men in our group and a man in a suit, who were now walking behind the group. *Oh well, another sucker is about to be taken advantage of,* I thought to myself.

While walking, one of the other men in our group nudged me with his elbow and raised his eyebrows a couple of times while nodding his head towards the blonde-haired woman. He was obviously as impressed with the blonde-haired woman's rather shapely derrière as I was.

"My name is Guy Purvis," he said.

"Hi, I'm Jake Douglas," I replied.

At six feet one inch, and probably about twenty-seven to twenty-eight years old, Guy was ruggedly handsome and well built. Based upon his remarks and stares, I tagged him as a lady's man whose sole task in life was to seduce every woman that caught his eye.

"Did you notice the nice rack?" he whispered, as he leaned towards me.

I had immediately checked out the blonde-haired woman as soon as she had walked into the cafeteria. I almost never missed a pretty woman and had my own numerical female rating system (FRS). It had been an idea, provided by the actor Steve McQueen, in the 1963 movie *Soldier in the Rain.*

McQueen's character, Eustis Clay, liked to rate women's shapes, and he had an alphabetical rating system from which I adopted my own. I realized that some, especially women, would not look upon this somewhat juvenile practice favorably. Therefore, I normally kept it entirely to myself and used it to pass the time as a form of self-entertainment.

"Yeah a FRS of 8.5," I whispered, as I nodded yes.

Guy gave me a quizzical look but did not say anything else, as we came to a room, whose wooden door was equipped with a large frosted glass center panel. The nice looking woman motioned us through the door. As we entered the long room, I saw there were five rows of the old, school-type, slide-in metal desks that had the small wooden desktops. Instantly, my mind raced back to my school years, and I recalled how uncomfortable those seats could be. *Oh well, this was going to be home for the next few weeks, at least during the days, so I might as well get used to it.* I moved towards the rear center of the room and sat down at one of the desks.

As I sat down in my desk, I noticed George Carriby struggle to sit down in the desk immediately to my right. After a somewhat halfhearted attempt to fit his mass into the small, uncomfortable desk, he simply stood up and smiled with a sheepish grin.

I thought I heard him mumble something like, "I ain't gonna git my big butt in anything like that."

As soon as all the people who came from the cafeteria had sat down in the room, three men dressed in suits entered the room and walked towards the front. I immediately recognized the three as part of the group of four men who had been previously sitting in the opposite corner of the cafeteria from me.

As one of the men stepped forward, he said in a commanding voice, "Good morning, class."

"Good morning," most of the people in the room replied.

"My name is John Dawson, and I'll be the Chief Training Officer for this Special Agent Class. I have been in the Air Force for ten years and previously worked in the legal field."

At that time, Dawson pointed to George and said, "Do you have a problem there, Sergeant?"

"Yes, sir," George replied in his best southern drawl.

"And what would that problem be?" Dawson asked.

"Well, sir, I don't seem to fit into this tiny little people's desk."

The majority of the students, as well as the three men in the front of the class, broke out in laughter.

"Yes, Sergeant, I can see that might in fact be a problem. Capt. Brown, can you see if you can find the Sergeant a better seating arrangement?"

"Sure thing, Capt. Dawson, I think we have a few slightly larger desks, just for this type of situation. I'll be back in a few minutes."

Capt. Brown returned shortly with a larger desk, and George was able to sit down.

"By the way," Capt. Dawson stated, "the woman who showed you to the classroom was Sherri Green. She is the school director's secretary. I should warn you, she is off limits, especially to students!"

"You may call me John, and I want to welcome you all to OSI, Washington, D.C. and this class of twenty-two students which, since it's the fourth class of the year, will become known as "Class D.""

The students themselves later named our class "Dawson's Dogs."

Dawson advised that, due to the tight class schedule, punctuality was important. John stated the course was the first of two schools for some of the students, since there were six prospective technical agents and sixteen prospective regular agents in this class.

All students would be required to complete this course, which was ten weeks long, and its focus would be on general investigative techniques. At that point, the regular agents would graduate and go out to their assignments to work in OSI.

"Would the six future technical agents please raise their hands?" John asked.

George and I raised our hands, and four others in the room raised theirs. I saw Guy Purvis had raised his hand along with Frank Kurgland, Skip Felton and one other person. In my effort to get into the room and find a good seat, I had lost track of Skip. I now noticed he was sitting over a couple of rows and towards the front of the room. That would be a good place for me to keep track of him so I would know what he was doing.

"The technical agents who are part of this class will be required to learn general investigative techniques and evidence collection so later, if they should discover a clandestine technical surveillance device, they would have the knowledge and skills to correctly preserve it and collect it as evidence," John said.

John went on to say that after the technical agents successfully completed this first course, they would then attend a second school that would last another six weeks. It would cover special technical investigative techniques. There could be a lengthy break between the schools.

"You regular agents will later come to appreciate the technical agents when they assist you with maybe video or audio surveillance techniques to help solve some of your cases. You will then learn why the technical agents are known within OSI as The Hobbyshop Boys. Their skills, techniques and equipment are extremely useful in collecting some of the more complex and difficult evidence."

According to John, the first course would consist of five two-week sections, and the group would be tested at the end of each section. A passing score was seventy-five percent. If a person failed a test for any section, they would be given the opportunity to go back to the next class, or "wash back," and retake that section. If a person failed more than one section, they would be eliminated from the school. The school's failure rate was approximately ten to fifteen percent.

I made another mental note to myself right then – **I certainly would not be one of the failures!**

"Another thing I should mention at this point," Said John, "is that by entering into the position of an OSI agent, you are placing yourselves in a position that gets extreme professional and personal scrutiny. You are joining the ranks of federal law enforcement officers and are hereafter expected to conduct yourselves in a manner of extreme personal discretion at all times. Everything you do will have to set the example for others in the Air Force, and any personal or professional errors or mistakes you make will put you in jeopardy of being discharged from your position in OSI.

"So, not only do you have to complete a very difficult training program but, from here on, you must live an exemplary life in the public eye. You will soon learn the unofficial motto of our organization: Discretion, Discretion, Discretion."

After John completed his presentation and introduced the other two men, Captains Frank Lander and James Brown as his training assistants, he stated he would like to introduce the director of the OSI School, Colonel Robert Tredorf. The colonel, who had entered the room in the rear, unnoticed by most of the group while John had been giving his speech, slowly walked to the front of the room. I recognized him as the fourth "suit" that had been at the corner table in the cafeteria.

"I'd like to extend my personal welcome to OSI and this course to each of you," said Tredorf. "Our agency is, simply put, the professional investigative arm for the Air Force. When it was created in 1948, it was structured after the Federal Bureau of Investigation. In fact, our first Commander, Brigadier General Joseph Terroll, was recruited as a special agent from the FBI and given the rank of General. We are proud of our heritage and work hard to retain the respect we have earned within the federal investigative community. We're responsible for the conduct of espionage, fraud, criminal and technical investigations in support of commanders within the Air Force."

"You people in this class that are going to be special agents will be assigned to one of the three major investigative branches.

"I understand we have six potential technical agents in this class. That's great, as we currently need more technical agents in OSI and are actively recruiting those personnel."

Tredorf said the course would be a little tough, as it presented a lot of information in a rather condensed format, but most people who had made it this far in the selection process would make it through the school. He stated his instructors were handpicked, very professional and personally motivated to assist each student to complete the course. If anyone had any special problems during the school, they were welcome to request to speak to him at any time. With that, he thanked the group for their willingness to devote themselves to the training required to become an OSI agent and stated, "Carry on."

After Col. Tredorf departed the room, John started going through the individual two-week class sections that were in front of the students. The first section would deal with an overview of the agency, its history, the other federal agencies with whom OSI worked, and their general methods and procedures and the general legal aspects of special investigations. The second section would consist of crime scene preservation, investigation, and the legal aspects of that entire process. The third section would consist of evidence collection techniques and photography. The fourth section would be devoted to more detailed physical evidence collection skills and practical exercises. The fifth section would deal with handling sources, surveillance techniques, physical surveillance exercises and an introduction to executive protection operations.

"I and the other two instructors will be the principal instructors for each section of the course," John said. "We will be assisted at various times by other OSI Headquarters personnel."

John then stated the class would now be given a twenty-minute break. We could either stay in the room or go back down the hall to the cafeteria. George and I stood up at the same time. I immediately noticed Skip had started walking towards the front of the room. *Ah, the kiss ass is already starting to work his magic,* I thought to myself.

George said, "Let's go get a cup of coffee."

"Sounds good to me," I said.

Just as we turned to leave the room, a third man who had held up his hand as a future technical agent said, "Hey that sounds good. Do you mind if I join you?"

"Not at all," I said, as I extended my right hand towards the man. "We technical agents have to stick together. My name is Jake Douglas."

"Jim Connel," said the man, as he shook my hand.

I had seen Jim around the barracks and on the bus but had not had the opportunity to talk to him yet. I was to learn later that Jim was everyone's friend. He was married, and his wife's name was Mary.

After I had known Jim for a while, I came to realize that while he might never become a leader, and probably had no desire for that, he was the rock steady worker everyone wanted to have with them and relied upon. Given proper directions, Jim was an excellent team player. Jim was slightly older than the rest of us, at about thirty years old. He had been in another branch of the U.S. military and, after some type of injury, had transferred to the Air Force.

George was right there with his hand, saying, "George Carriby. Did I hear you say your name is Jim?"

"Yes, Jim Connel. Glad to meet you George."

As we walked out of the classroom, Jim turned to George.

"So, with that deep drawl, George, where you from, and what did you do before this?" asked Jim.

"My home is near Austin, Texas," replied George. "And I was in radio maintenance."

"How about you, Jim, where you from, and what did you do?" inquired George.

"Oh, I'm from Panama City, Florida," stated Jim, "and I was in radar maintenance."

"I thought OSI only recruited people for technical services out of the radio maintenance field," said George.

"Yeah, that's where they always look first, I'm told, but they do take a few other electronics maintenance types. I've already been advised I will have to cross train into the radio maintenance field."

"Well, I'll be darned. You learn something new every day," said George.

As we were walking down the hall, Guy Purvis, who I had spoken to earlier on the way to the classroom, joined us.

"Hello, Guy," I stated. "I'm glad to see you are one of us technical types."

"George and Jim, this is Guy Purvis. He and I met earlier this morning."

"Yeah, we were both checking out Sherri Green's rather fine butt," said Guy.

"I don't think any man in the cafeteria or the hallway missed taking a look at that fine shapely woman," Jim said. "Nice to meet you Guy."

"Now that is a natural fact," stated George. "Good to know you, Guy."

Jim looked at Guy and me and asked, "What did you two do in the regular Air Force, and where are you from?"

"I worked in radio maintenance," I replied "and I'm from Tulsa, Oklahoma.

"I wasn't in the Air Force," replied Guy. "I was in the Navy and worked in electronics maintenance. I'm from Ithaca, New York."

"Ah, a Squid," I said. "No wonder you're horny."

As we entered the cafeteria and walked over to the coffee urns, Guy turned to me and said, "Alright Jake, you've really got my curiosity up. What's FRS?"

I chuckled and said, "That's my own personal rating system for women."

Guy smiled and asked, "You've got a system for rating women? Hell, boy, I thought I was the only guy that rated women!"

"Not on your life," I said.

"OK, OK, man, you've got to fill me in on this FRS. First of all, what does FRS mean?"

"Well, FRS simply means female rating system."

"Didn't you watch the movie *Soldier in the Rain* with Steve McQueen?"

"Yes. So you mean that's how it works?" said Guy.

I sat down at one of the empty tables with my coffee, and the other three men joined me.

"I make it a point to observe every woman that I see. And I don't mean just look at them. I study them as close as time will allow.

"When I have given the lady my full review, I then give her a female rating, which is a number from one to ten, one being the lowest and ten being the highest."

"So, you gave Sherri a rating of eight point five," moaned Guy. "What are you, crazy? Man, she is gorgeous and, under your system, I'd give her a ten!"

George and Jim both chimed in at the same time, "Yeah, man, she is a beauty!"

"Well, guys, it is my rating system after all, so I will call them as I see them!"

George looked down at his watch and then looked around the cafeteria. "Hey, guys, I think we're late for getting back to class."

"Oh, great," said Jim who turned out to be a worrier, "Our first day, and we start by taking too long for the break."

"Get over it," said Guy," We're going to be living here for the next ten weeks, a few minutes can't be all that bad."

As we walked back to the classroom, Guy looked at Jake and stated, "Man, she has to be at least a nine, and you're blind and too hard of a judge! Besides that, I'll let you know how good she is within two weeks!"

"Are you crazy?" said George, "You heard John. She's the director's secretary. How do you propose to even get near her?"

"That might be the hardest part," said Guy, "but I have my own approach technique that works a high percentage of the time."

"Haven't you learned the first rule about dating someone where you work?" I asked.

"And what rule would that be?" asked Guy.

"Oh, I don't know. It goes something like, don't dip your pen into company ink," I replied.

"That's so dated," said Guy, "Besides; it only matters if you get caught!"

"And what about that unofficial OSI motto of Discretion, Discretion, Discretion," I asked.

"Oh, that. I've already made a slight change to that motto."

"Yeah, and what would that be?" asked Jim.

"How about – Discretion, Discretion, Discretion, Deny, Deny, Deny!"

"Wow, that didn't take you long to make a significant change in an old organizational motto," stated George.

"Yeah, I tend to make little changes to things when I think it better suits my needs," replied Guy.

"Well, you'd better be careful with that habit, or you might not be in this organization very long," I advised. "By the way, I'll put twenty dollars on the two-week timeframe," I said.

"You're on," laughed Guy.

"Hey, I want a piece of that action," said Jim. "I'll put twenty dollars on that also."

"OK, I'll be more than glad to take some Florida money along with that Oklahoma money. How about you George? You want in on this?"

"Nah, not me man, I don't gamble unless it's a sure thing, and you squids are known for getting the women!"

"Smart move George."

That was my first of many lessons on learning just how "tight" George was. I soon accused him of squeaking when he walked and told him that every time he opened his wallet, moths flew out of it!

"How are you going to prove that you made the conquest?" asked Jim.

"We'll discuss that later," said Guy as he opened the classroom door, and they stepped into a class already in session.

CHAPTER 3

"Glad you could join us, Jake," a voice said, as we entered the room. It was Skip Felton. I had noticed he was sitting near the door when we left the classroom but had somehow forgotten about him. He grabbed the opportunity to call special attention to me, and the others with me, by loudly announcing our late arrival back to the class, as if that had really been necessary. John Dawson had looked directly at us as soon as we had entered the door.

Immediately John said, "Will the four gentlemen that just entered please see me after this class?" John was obviously not pleased by the interruption.

"Yes, sir," we all replied simultaneously.

Skip was someone I only tolerated in public, and then only if necessary. Skip had always used and abused anything and anyone in his effort to get ahead in any situation. I hated that about him and had confronted him about it on several occasions. We had physically fought on a couple of occasions, but nothing I'd found to date could make him change his ways. He just did not care about what he had to do to make himself look good. I might have seriously reconsidered attending this class date if I had known Skip would be here. It was bad enough my new friends and I were late returning from the first class break, but to have Skip sitting there by the entrance door and calling extra attention to it was just bad luck.

Skip was basically a jerk! He was lucky though and often seemed to come out on top of most situations.

"As I was just explaining," John said, "this building will be your primary location for the training you'll be involved in during the next ten weeks. However, your billets will be located on Bolling

23

AFB. You'll travel between the two locations each day by bus. You must be through with your morning activities each day by 7:40 am, at which time, you'll board the bus outside your billets for the ride here. You will be provided lunch each day, here at the cafeteria. Your breakfast and dinners will be provided at the chow hall on Bolling. Classes will begin *promptly* each weekday morning at 8:00 am."

I could not help but notice the inflection in John's voice on the word promptly and the glance from Skip.

"On the weekends, you'll have some free time, but you'll also be expected to participate in some practical exercises, and I'm sure you'll be studying a lot," John went on to say.

"Alright, gentlemen, we'll now get into the first section of your OSI training course. As I mentioned earlier today, this section will involve the history of OSI, its interaction with other federal agencies and general investigative techniques used by OSI personnel. The first portion of this week will be taught by Capt. Frank Lander," John said, as he motioned to Frank who had been sitting in the front row.

Frank stood up, and moved to the front center of the room. He introduced himself and said that he had been in the Air Force for nine years and had previously worked in the security police. He was tall and stood straight in good military bearing. He had a pleasant look and a warm smile.

The rest of the morning was uneventful and filled with somewhat dry lecture, viewgraphs and videos of the organization, its history and its mission. Then each of the three major branches of OSI came and gave an overview of their branches and individual missions. And then a technical agent, named Ralph Cuber, came and wowed everyone with what I was to learn later was called the "Dancing Bear Show." It was a demonstration of some of the equipment technical agents used and then a lock picking demonstration. We technical types were to learn later that Ralph was one of the technical personnel actually assigned to the OSI Headquarters Technical Services Division. He was very well known within TSD and very highly thought of. We also learned the people at Headquarters TSD did not normally do the fieldwork that we "common folk" had to do. While they all had served in the field, they, as all other headquarters types, were responsible for controlling the fieldwork not actually doing it. Of course, that sometimes led to misunderstandings between the headquarters personnel and the field workers.

After the class, Jim, George, Guy and I met with John. He started by advising us, in a very serious voice, that we had certainly not gotten off to a good start in this training course.

He stated that, due to the nature of this training and the pressure placed upon the school to turn out quality personnel, he should bounce us all from the course immediately. He asked if we thought we should be given a second chance. I took the initiative as a group spokesman and told him that, in the excitement of the moment, we had just gotten carried away and let time slip by without noticing how long we had been on break. We each, in turn, replied we would not let this happen again. John emphasized we must be punctual in the future, or we would be sent packing without question.

We had one more uneventful ten-minute break during the morning and, then at 11:30 am, the class broke for lunch.

As the class started getting up, I had anticipated the announcement and had moved quickly to get over to Skip as he was opening the classroom door.

"Thanks for the publicity, you brown-nosing jerk," I grunted to Skip.

"Think nothing of it, you goodie-two shoes," hissed Skip. "I was sorry to see you here."

"The feeling is mutual, I assure you," I said.

By now, George, Jim and Guy had joined me for the walk to the cafeteria. Jim was the first to ask, "What is up with that guy, and who is he?"

"Don't worry about him," I advised, "He and I go back a long way in radio maintenance, and most of it has been less than friendly."

"I'll handle him later."

"He has always been a jerk, and one to climb the ladder of life by stepping on others."

As we entered the cafeteria, Guy was the first to notice Sherri was already there and sitting with Col. Tredorf. "Damn," he muttered as he eyed her with a lustful stare. We all got our meal, and Guy managed to get a table with a clear view of Sherri.

The remainder of the first two-week section of the school was spent getting guest lectures. Those lectures were from the Federal Bureau of Investigation (FBI); the Drug Enforcement Administration (DEA); Alcohol, Tobacco & Firearms (ATF); the Central Intelligence Agency (CIA); the Defense Intelligence Agency (DIA); the Office of Naval Investigations (ONI); the Criminal Investigations Division (CID); the Postal Investigations Department; the U.S. Customs & Immigration Service; and the National Security Administration (NSA). Each agency brought their own "dog & pony show" to inform the students what their particular agency's mission was and where the OSI fit in with their joint-support missions.

Also during this section, the class was further introduced to the second assistant trainer Captain James Brown who had been in the Air Force for nine years and came from the security police. The assistant director of the OSI School, Wilbur Owens, was also introduced. He was a civilian and had worked in OSI for fifteen years. We were also enlightened with the very boring, but completely necessary, classes on the legal aspects and criminal law requirements of special investigations. Those were the hardest classes to remain awake in and the hardest subject matter on the section test. Jim Connell had struggled hard with the legal aspects and the criminal law information, which was all new to him and not easy to grasp and retain. I had been able to pick up on these subjects easier than he had, so I spent several evenings tutoring him on these subjects.

"So, Jim, why is this legal stuff so hard for you to grasp?" I asked.

"I'm not sure, Jake. It's just so dry, and there's so many 'if this, then that,' and 'the penal system this, and criminal law section that.' I just really don't like it!"

"Well, I understand and feel the same way, but if you want to pass this section of the school, you have to learn and retain this legal stuff at least long enough to pass the test."

"Yeah, I know. I'll just go over it until I memorize it."

"Call your wife, Mary, and talk to her. That will settle you down. How long have you two been married?"

"Nine years and two months. I haven't been away from her for this long very often and am finding it very difficult. I do not do very well without her. She makes a lot of decisions for me, and I rely upon her more than I realized."

"How many children do you have?"

"We have one boy, seven, and one girl, five".

"And they're all down in Florida while you're here?" I asked.

"Yes, Mary went back to Panama City to visit her parents while I'm in school. You know, when you're in the military, you don't get to spend much time at home. I've tried to get stationed at Tyndall Air Force Base many times so we could be close to home, but so far it hasn't happened."

"Well, I hear we have a technical division at Patrick Air Force Base, so maybe you can put in for it when we get a chance to request an assignment here in school."

"Yes, I plan to try. I think that I'll go call her now."

Jim left the barracks to go call his wife. "Hello, sweetheart, I miss you and wanted to hear your voice."

"I miss you too, Jim. Things just don't seem the same without you."

"How are you and the kids doing?"

"Oh, we're getting by alright. Dad and Mom have been very good to us and have taken us to the beach several times. The kids really like that. How are you?"

"Me, I'm doing OK, but I'm having a rough time with this section of the school. There's a whole lot of stuff on criminal law and the penal system, and I'm finding it so hard to remember."

"Well, honey, I wish I was there to help you. Is anyone there who can help you?"

"Yes, I've met this guy named Jake, and he's helping me a lot. We've been studying together in the evenings and on the weekends."

"Well, you study hard and just memorize the material for the test. I know that you can do it, Jim. Remember how much you want to have this new job."

"Yes, I know, and that's what is getting me through this school. I just miss having you around to help me with things," Jim said.

"I know, but you'll do fine. I'm glad Jake is helping you. Have you made any other friends there?"

"Yes, there are four of us guys that hang out together. Besides Jake, there is Guy Purvis and George Carriby."

"It sounds like you're doing alright. Take care, and call me again soon."

"OK, I love you," Mary said.

"Yes, I love you, too."

Jim managed to squeak through the dreaded test with a minimum score. Not everyone passed the test though. There were two failures, both of which were regular agents. They chose to wash back to the next class and try again.

During the first two-week section of the school, the subject of Guy getting together with Sherri came up in conversation.

"So," Jim asked Guy one morning as we were all eating breakfast, "have you decided how you are going to prove that you got together with Sherri?"

"How about just getting her to write you a note stating I messed around with Guy," said George, and they all busted out laughing.

The rest of the people in the chow hall looked annoyed at the sudden outburst of noise coming from our group that had become known for such antics.

"I'll tell you what," said Guy, "after I have conquered said damsel, I'll personally go over to her table in the cafeteria and get her to blush openly. Would that satisfy your requirements, my liege?"

"That ought to do the job," I answered.

By now, the rest of our little group had pretty well figured Guy out. He was definitely the ladies' man – at least in his own mind. And, to hear him tell stories of his time in the Navy, he could have well been the person Ricky Nelson was singing about in his song "Traveling Man." He had obviously always done well with women and did not mind talking about it. According to him, he had several girls asking him to take them to the high school prom, and he tried to arrange to take them all.

CHAPTER 4

On the fourth day of the first week, Captain Brown was the only instructor in the class at one point, and he needed to have the assistant school director come to the classroom for a particular reason. Guy had just been waiting for an unexpected opportunity to arise and give him a reason to penetrate the "holy ground" of the Director's Office Complex. Guy sensed that Brown needed something and was looking nervously around the classroom. When Brown suddenly asked if anyone could possibly go to the Director's Complex and request Mr. Owens to come to the classroom, Guy was up and moving towards the door, before he even started to answer with his, "I'd be happy to go, sir!"

As he later told the group, when he entered the complex, Sherri was sitting alone in the outer office, and the door to Owens' office was closed.

He told her he had been requested to bring Mr. Owens to the classroom. She told him that Owens had someone in his office at the moment, and asked if he would care to wait. On the other hand, she could just tell Owens he was needed.

"No problem," Guy replied. "I'll wait."

He had instantly noticed she was not wearing a wedding ring, although that would not have stopped his next move.

"I'm Guy Purvis, and I already know you are Sherri Green."

"And I know who you are," she replied coyly.

Guy knew this was his moment and did not know how long it would last before Owens' door would open or Col. Tredorf might call for Sherri. Therefore, it was the moment for his approach technique. It was one that, while particularly crude and blunt, had worked well for him many times, as it was direct, to the point and caught the targeted damsel completely off guard.

As he looked down at her, he focused on her blue eyes and asked, "Do you mess around?"

The flush in her face was immediate, and he knew then he had given Jake the correct signal to look for. She sucked in a sharp breath and was obviously taken back.

She started to stammer momentarily and, just as she looked him directly in the eyes and softly said "sometimes," the door to Owens' office opened and a person started to slowly back out as he continued to provide an answer to Mr. Owens.

"Meet me at the entrance to the National Gallery of Art, downtown at 10:30 am Saturday morning," Guy quickly whispered to her.

"OK," was all she had time to say.

At that moment, Owens followed the departing man out of his office, looked at Sherri, who was still slightly blushing, focused his stare on Guy and gruffly asked, "What do you want here?"

Guy could hardly get his voice to come out of his mouth and, for a second or two, all he could do was clear his throat.

"Mr. Brown asked me to come and get you sir," he finally managed to say in a weak voice.

"Oh, well, tell him I'll be right there."

"Yes, sir," replied Guy, as he nervously glanced down at the now smiling Sherri and bumped into the doorjamb on his way out of the room.

My God, that was close Guy thought to himself as he slowly made his way back to the classroom. *Damn, I'm good,* he complimented himself next, as he opened the door and said to Mr. Brown, "Mr. Owens will be here in a moment, sir."

As he made his way back to his chair, Guy couldn't help but feel the stares of Jake, George and Jim, and he knew without any doubt exactly what they were thinking. All he had time to do, before he slid into his desk, was raise his right hand slightly with his thumb pointing up.

He was immediately aware of a muffled word from me that sounded something like, "Bull."

At the next break, the three of us were all over Guy for an explanation of what he had meant by the thumbs up. Guy went through the description of his trip to the Directors' Complex with slow, excruciating details.

"Come on, get to the good part," whined Jim.

"Well, since I knew this had to be my chance and Sherri was just sitting there all alone, and I couldn't get into Owens' Office right away, I simply introduced myself to her."

"Yeah, what did she say?" asked George.

She said, "Yeah I know who you are!"

"Bull," once again came out of my mouth.

"I kid you not," said Guy. "She obviously knows a good thing when she sees it!"

"So what happened then?" I requested.

"Well again, I knew that I didn't have much time, so I decided to just go for it," replied Guy. "I slid over a little closer to her desk and hit her with my approach technique!"

"Ok, Ok, what is it?" asked Jim.

"I told you guys that I have a good approach technique and that it often works for me."

"Would you just get to it?" George was getting impatient.

"I looked into her eyes, and I said, 'Do you mess around?'"

"That's it!" I cried, "That's what you said?"

"Yeah, that is my approach technique! Sometimes I get slapped, and sometimes I get lucky!"

"Just like that, you come out with that blunt, crude, direct question, and it works?" queried Jim.

"That's it! I'm going to meet her Saturday morning at the National Gallery of Art."

"What? You're going to meet her at the Art Gallery?" asked George.

"Not bad, man, not bad," I said. "You have a real touch of class. How did you know she would like the art gallery?"

"Quick guess," said Guy, "She had a nice Hudson River School print called *In the Catskills* by Thomas Doughty on the wall behind her.

"Anyway, I'll be seeing her in the cafeteria early next week, so be sure to have my money, Jake!"

That evening, I visited Guy's room to talk to him and get to know him a little better.

"Hey, Guy, mind if I come in?" I asked

"Not at all, what can I do for you?"

"Nothing special, I just wanted to visit for a while before it gets too late. Where did you say you are from?"

"Ithaca, New York," Guy stated

"Is that in the upstate area or down near the city. I've never been in New York."

"It's in about the center of the southern portion, upstate. It's very pretty country. You should visit there some time."

"Yeah, I've always wanted to see upstate New York and the Niagara Falls area."

So, are you married?" I asked.

"Was twice, but being in the Navy isn't always good for marriages. I was gone too much. So now, I just try to stay with 'one nighters' or limited engagements."

"Did you do a lot of Sea Duty?"

"Yeah, we would be out about six months at a time."

"What exactly did you do?"

"I worked in Submarines. It was great duty at first, but it got old."

"How about you, Jake? Have you been married?" Guy asked.

"No, I haven't found the right one yet."

We talked for about another half an hour, and then I headed off to bed.

Monday morning, of the second two-week section, as the students were getting on the bus, George, Jim and I were looking around for Guy.

"Did you see him at all this weekend?" asked George.

Jim and I just shook our heads no. As the last person was getting on the bus, Guy ran out of the barrack and was hollering, "Hold the bus." He climbed up the steps and made his way back to the empty seat I was saving for him. The other two men of our group were sitting in the seat behind us, and immediately Jim looked at Guy with a big grin and said, "Well?"

"Let me catch my breath," said Guy.

"You don't look any different," stated George.

"Maybe not," said Guy, "but I'm breathing so much better!"

"What does that mean?" asked Jim.

"Well, after a wild weekend, it is amazing how much lighter my chest is and how much easier it is for me to breath! By the way, Jake, I hope you have my money. I'll collect it the first time we see Sherri alone in the cafeteria."

"Tell us all about it," begged George.

"Hey, I'm not the type to kiss and tell."

"Bull," I quipped, "you can't wait to give us all of the slimy details."

"That's not nice," said Guy. "Show a little respect for said young damsel."

"Just get on with it man," stated Jim.

"Well, we met at 10:30 am sharp at the National Gallery of Art. I took a cab downtown and got out about a half a block away from the building. I wanted to make sure no one was following me and that the coast was clear at the Gallery. When I got about fifty yards from the building, I could see Sherri standing at the bottom of the steps and all alone. I looked around the whole scene and didn't see anyone who looked out of place or particularly interested in her. I slowly walked up to her from behind and said, "Hello, I wasn't sure you'd be here."

"Why, I said OK, didn't I?" she replied.

"Yeah, but still I wasn't sure you would be here. By the way, why did you agree to such a direct approach?" asked Guy.

"Why not?" she said, "No one has ever asked me out quite like that. In fact, no one from the school has ever asked me out!"

34

"That's because all of the permanent personnel there don't have the nerve to ask you out, and the students are all told that you are 'off limits!'"

"Really," she said, "That explains why the students all seem to go out of their way to avoid me. Then why did you ask me out?" Sherry inquired.

In his best 'want to' voice, he said, "Because you really turn me on!"

"We'll see about that later," she said, "right now you brought me to the one place in D.C. I truly love and am surprised you enjoy, too."

"Beautiful women aren't all I enjoy," he replied, as they started up the steps. She giggled as she reached for his hand.

"Get out of here," said Jim, "you mean it was really that easy?"

"Go on," said George.

"We spent five hours in the art gallery then strolled around the National Mall. We went to Alexandria for dinner and then spent the rest of the weekend at her place," Guy said. "Man, I'll tell you. That woman must not have had any loving for quite some time! She's a tiger. We hardly took time to shower and eat."

All of the time this conversation was taking place, the bus had been rumbling out of the Main Gate of BAFB, and it now turned onto Interstate 295 north, as it made its way toward D.C.

"Skirt Alert! It's a real good one," cried someone in the rear of the bus. Immediately, everyone on the left side of the bus turned to look back so they could get the full, long view as the woman with the short skirt was passing.

It had not taken the students very long, once we had begun riding the bus from Bolling AFB to the Tempo E Building, to start observing the women with short skirts who were riding in the cars that passed the bus. Some of the women rode with their skirts up high to start with, and some seemed to take great delight in hiking their skirts up even further when they saw the bus with a lot of military guys.

There was usually a big rush in the mornings by the guys to get in the front of the bus line so they could sit in the left seats. The guys who had to sit on the right side of the bus always looked at the lucky ones in the left seats with a scowl on their face.

"Hot Darned," cried several of the guys, as the car slowly made its way past their view. It had become top priority for anyone sitting on the left rear of the bus to always let the others know when there was a short skirt approaching from the rear.

"Here comes another one!" yelled someone else.

"Oh wow," another set of voices said.

By now, the bus was on one of the city streets near the National Mall.

Suddenly, someone noticed a very shapely woman walking on the sidewalk ahead of the bus. The call went out, "Nice woman on the left walking."

"Would you look at the shape of that one?"

The woman was walking with a very large man. At about that time, I hollered out, "Yeah, but would you look at the size of that skirt protector!"

The whole bus laughed out loud and another new slang term was given birth!

CHAPTER 5

As we started the second two-week section of school, things started getting a lot more interesting. The first day consisted of a detailed discussion on what is involved in a crime scene preservation and investigation. John taught this portion of the school.

"I just want to remind you technical personnel that, although you wouldn't normally be involved in the collection of evidence, it's important for you, and anyone entering a crime scene, to be versed in the preservation and investigation of that location. This is so that any evidence existing at the scene of a crime remains intact and undisturbed until it can be properly photographed, preserved, collected and cataloged. All of this action is paramount to the legal procedures needed to insure all evidence is correctly obtained and can therefore be properly used in a court of law," said John.

No one in the class had any problem learning this subject, as we expected it would be very interesting.

At slightly past mid-morning, it was past time for our normal break. We had been retained in class by John to finish up on some of the legal aspects of evidence collection. When we did go on break, the cafeteria was almost empty, but Sherri was sitting all alone at a table in the back of the room.

After we got our coffee and donuts, we moved to a table close enough to Sherri to see her plainly, but not so close that it infringed upon her space.

As soon as the three other guys sat down, Guy walked over to her, bent down close to her ear and whispered something. She immediately turned a bright red. Guy gently touched her cheek, turned, and walked back to the table. At that time, Sherri got up and departed the cafeteria.

As he sat down, I covertly slipped him a twenty-dollar bill. "Thanks," said Guy, "that just makes it even sweeter."

"I'll get the money to you later," Jim said quietly.

After entering the cafeteria and being so involved in watching Guy and Sherri, I hadn't noticed Skip Felton come into the room and sit down away from us but with a clear view of our table. After Guy had gone over to where Sherri was sitting and then returned to our table, Skip made his move.

"Alright, Jake, what's going on? You know we were warned to stay away from Miss Green. Is this something I should bring to John's attention?"

All of us looked at Skip with disbelief and I'm sure a worried look. However, before any of the rest of us could gather our senses, George stood up and calmly looked down directly into Skip's eyes.

"If I even think it looks like you've said anything to anyone, I'll see to it personally that you are found floating in the Potomac River the next morning with a Texas necktie. Do you understand me?"

"Ye – yes, I understand. I won't mention it to anyone I promise." Skip turned pale and then hurried out of the room and did not look back.

After he left, Guy turned to George and said, "Thanks George. By the way, what is a Texas necktie?"

"Aw, you know, it's one of those tied up rope things."

"You mean a noose?" I asked

"Yeah, I didn't remember what that was called."

The rest of us chuckled at that.

When we returned to class, Skip was seated and didn't even look at us when we entered. Frank Lander was there to get us started in the practical session of working a crime scene search.

"These are photos of real crime scenes," Frank stated as he handed out sets of photographs. "Each set of photos show different views of the same crime scene. Please look over the photo sets carefully. Each of you are to analyze the photos and then write down everything you notice, in each photo, that appears to be evidence or is obviously out of place. When you are through making your notes, put your name on them. Then please hand in the notes and the photos, and it will be time for lunch. After lunch, I will hand back your notes and photos, and we will review each set and discuss the evidence you should have noted in the photos."

During lunch, the entire class was buzzing about what we had observed and what we thought was evidence.

When the class convened again, the photos and notes were handed back to each student. Frank then started around the room, calling on one student at a time and asking what one item they noted as being probable evidence and/or out of place.

Several of the students had correctly picked each piece of evidence and the things that looked out of place in the photos. Most photos were of material crime scenes only, but some of them contained bodies.

That evening, George seemed to be deep in thought and off in a world of his own. I didn't say much as we walked up to the chow hall for dinner, figuring it best to leave him alone. He would probably talk when he was ready. After dinner, as we walked back to the barracks, George cleared his throat.

"Jake, can we juz walk for a while. I need to get something off my chest."

"Sure, George, what's up?"

"Well, Molly has been having some medical problems. I'm really torn on what I should do."

"What's wrong with her?" I asked.

"Oh, she hasn't been handling things very well. I guess she's under a lot of stress because George Jr. has been having problems at school and has been misbehaving."

"It sounds to me like they both have just been missing you a lot, and don't know how to handle it. Has Molly talked to Jr.'s teacher to see what they may think the problem could be?"

"Yeah, and the teacher has said about the same thing as you just did."

"Sounds to me like you just need to call them tonight and talk to both of them for quite some time. Let them know that you're missing them as much as they're missing you and that you'll be home soon with a new job."

"Yeah, that sounds like a good idea. I think I'll do juz that. Do you mind going back to the barracks by yourself?"

"Not at all, you go make your call, and I'll see you later."

Later that evening, George made it back to our room and said that he had talked to Molly and Jr., and things were better with both of them.

CHAPTER 6

The next phase of this training section involved teaching the students actual evidence collection techniques. First would be how to identify, then mark off and protect a crime scene.

The students were taken to a different section of the building for some practical exercises in identifying and protecting a potential crime scene. The students were placed in four-person groups with a team leader identified by John.

The purpose of the exercise was for the team to respond to a possible crime, determine if in fact a crime had been committed, identify the possible crime scene and mark it off to protect any potential evidence. For our team, Jim was selected as the team leader for the first exercise. Our team was told to respond to a possible breaking and entering of an on-base store.

The alarm system had gone off at the location, and the manager had been notified and was on his way. The security police had responded and reported that it appeared a rear door had been forced open.

As the team was going to the potential crime scene, Jim told us that we should begin looking around the area once we got there to see if we could find anything out of place.

The team responded to the location and found two men (with S.P. taped to their hats) there, at what was supposed to be the rear door of the business.

"Have either of you two officers entered the business?" Jim asked.

Both officers stated they hadn't, as they didn't want to disturb a crime scene.

At that time, the owner of the business arrived and wanted to enter the building.

"Pardon me, sir, my name is Special Investigator Connel. Are you the manager of the store?"

"Yes, Mr. Connel, my name is George Smith."

"May I see your identification, sir?" Jim asked.

"Is that really necessary, Mr. Connel?"

"Yes, I have to be sure of who you are before I proceed," Jim replied.

"No one has gone into the store yet, as the perpetrators may still be in there. Therefore, I can't allow you to enter at this time. Can you verify that the rear door had been secured when you departed the store today?"

Mr. Smith replied, "Yes, I personally secured the door from the inside before I closed this evening. Due to the type of locking devices I use, it would be impossible for anyone to have entered the door from the outside without a forced entry."

"Thank you, sir," Jim replied.

Based upon the information provided by Mr. Smith, Jim made the determination that this was a probable crime scene by forced entry, which met the requirements for a breaking and entering violation of the criminal code.

At this point, Jim requested the two police officers to clear the store and reminded them not to disturb any potential evidence, if possible, to include not touching the door handle as they entered the building. In a few minutes, the officers came back out of the building and advised the business was clear.

At those words, the store manager wanted to enter the building, but Jim stopped him again and said, "I know you're concerned about the status of your business, sir, but I can't let you go in there until the OSI investigators have been allowed to collect and preserve any possible evidence. As soon as we are through collecting any evidence, you will be allowed to enter your business."

At that point, Jim told the rest of us team members to go on into the building and begin collecting evidence.

Right about then, John Dawson appeared at the scene. "Is your team through with the exercise?" he asked.

"Yes, sir, I believe we are," Jim replied.

John then told the team to go back to the training room where we would be critiqued.

After we returned to the classroom, John followed a short while later.

"How do you think you did on the exercise?" John asked.

The whole team answered, "Good," at the same time.

"Jim, do you recall the pre-exercise instructions?" John inquired.

"Yes, I do, and in fact I have them written down," Jim replied.

"Do you remember what had been said about the hallway where the exercise had taken place?" he asked.

Jim took a second to look at his notes and then softly moaned, "Oh no."

"What's the matter?" I asked.

"The hallway," Jim muttered, "it was part of the potential crime scene!" Looking at John, he said, "Don't tell me there was evidence there?"

"Was there?" asked John. "Apparently you don't know, do you? What do you think? If that was the alley behind a business that had a forced entry, could there have been evidence left behind?"

"Yes, of course," Jim replied. "We were just in such a hurry to get to the scene that we simply didn't stop to think about looking in the alley."

"Believe me, you certainly aren't the first group to pull a bone-headed stunt like that!" said John. "If you had looked, you might have found shoeprints in a muddy area near the rear door of the business. You might have also found a steel bar that may have been the forced entry tool, as well as possible fingerprints on it. Now, I realize you were not specifically looking for evidence during this exercise; however, you were supposed to determine if a crime had occurred and, if so, protect the crime scene. Overall, you did a very good job for your first crime scene," stated John.

"Thank you, sir," Jim replied.

The three other teams all had about the same luck on their first crime scene. The remainder of the team leaders each completed their tasks in a similar manner, and all teams received good training and experience from the exercises.

The rest of the second, two-week section went on without much fanfare. As before, the legal aspect of crime scene preservation and investigation was boring to all except to a few of the people with a law background. Everyone completed the second examination satisfactorily. I again had tutored Jim with some of the legal aspects.

It was during this time that the other technical agents and I went downstairs to the Technical Services Directorate to visit with the two headquarters technical agents that worked in the electronics lab. We wanted to hear from them about what we might expect to do when we actually were assigned to a District Office in the field.

As we walked into the lab, one of the agents met us.

"Hello, can I help you?" the man said with a deep southern drawl.

"Yes, my name is Jake Douglass, and these are the other potential technical agents who are in the 69-D Basic Class upstairs. This is George Carriby, Frank Kurgland, Guy Purvis, Jim Connell and Skip Felton. We would just like to talk to you about what you do here and what we can expect when we get to the field."

"Hi, my name is Lenny Boyd. I am one of the two agents who currently work here in the electronics lab. The other guy isn't here right now, but his name is Bob Demar. Due to the fact that you are currently in training and may not complete the school, I cannot tell you as much as you may want to know at this time. However, I will tell you what I can."

"Thanks, we appreciate anything you can tell us. As I'm sure you are aware, we are wondering what we will do once we get to the field."

"Yes, we get this from every class that has potential technical agents."

Lenny was able to show us a few of the generic pieces of equipment that were used in the field such as some of the commercial video cameras, recorders and monitors and a few other non-sensitive items.

He was also able to give us a brief idea of what some of our jobs might entail. He gave us a good description of what we might be called upon to do in the conduct of some of the technical support operations such as collecting video and/or audio evidence to assist regular agents in support of a criminal or fraud investigation. He was able to give us a layman's idea of what the audio countermeasures surveys could entail.

"Unfortunately, that's about all I can tell you right now. As you get further along in your training, come back, and I will be able to explain more to you," he said.

We all thanked him for his time and for explaining what he could and told him that we would certainly be back later.

We headed back to class feeling much better about what lay ahead for us.

The next portion of our training would be to conduct a full crime-scene search and evidence collection, and the entire class was really looking forward to it.

It had been a long tough second, two-week portion of the training, and everyone was ready to let off some steam. Those who lived close enough would go home for the weekend. Those that didn't would have to make do in the local area. George and I grabbed a bite to eat after class and decided to go to the Electric Moon later, which was the closest Disco Dance Hall. I caught the look on George's face and laughed.

"I know if it ain't country music, it ain't music." I did my best imitation of my friend's Texas drawl.

"You know it, buddy," said George. "But I have to admit there are more pretty girls at the Electric Moon than at the Silver Stallion Bar. Besides, I'm kind of getting into to that Creedence stuff."

We headed back to our barracks. After getting cleaned up, I pulled on a pair of khaki slacks and a light blue shirt that brought out the color of my eyes. At least that's what I was told when I wore that shirt.

As we pulled into the parking lot at the Electric Moon, I glanced at the clock in my car's dash. It was only 8:00 pm. There weren't many cars in the lot, and I knew it would be a couple of hours before the joint starting jumping. As we entered the door, which led into a large rectangular building with a huge dance floor in the middle, we saw Jim sitting in a booth along the dance floor. As we got to the booth, a waitress met us. The good part about getting there early was you at least got some service. Later in the night, it wouldn't be the same!

"What'll you have, honey?" she asked.

"How about a JD and water – tall?" I figured it might be a long night, so there wasn't any sense in starting too hard.

"I'll take the same," said George.

"What are you doing here?" I asked Jim.

"Got a hankering to listen to some good music," he said.

"Seems like we all had the same thought," I replied. "I guess school is getting us all down. It's starting to get pretty interesting though."

"Yes, I definitely liked the evidence collection," George said.

We continued with the small talk about the school and how things were going. The bar started to slowly fill up, and there were now quite a few people drifting in. At 9:00 pm, the band started playing, and it suddenly became very loud in the bar. As usual, during the first two or three songs, no one got out on the dance floor.

I had been checking out the various women as they came into the bar. I had been watching a few of them and had narrowed my choices down to one or two. As I got up to go ask one of them to dance, another man suddenly appeared and walked straight up to her.

There was nothing to do but go to the head so as not to look like I had been going for the woman who had just been taken! There's nothing worse than to be out-maneuvered.

When I returned to the booth, both Jim and George gave me a silly grin.

George looked out on the dance floor and stated, "Weren't fast enough, were you?"

"Yeah, doesn't that just make you feel like you could walk up a snake's butt with a top hat on?" I asked.

"What are you doing going for that female when there are certainly better looking ones here tonight?" Jim asked.

"Just figured that I had a better chance of getting her to dance than the others," I said.

I waited the "required" two more songs before I got up again, just as the band started playing "Bad Moon Rising" by Creedence Clearwater Revival. I looked directly at the woman and walked straight towards her.

"Would you like to dance?" I said.

"Yes, I would like to dance with you."

"My name is Jake. What's yours?"

"Darlene," she replied.

We danced through the song with some more small talk. She asked me if I was from around the area, and I said that I was staying at Bolling AFB. The song ended, and the band started playing "You've Lost That Loving Feeling" by the Righteous Brothers.

"Care for a slow dance?" I asked.

"I would like that very much."

When the song was over, I asked her if she would care to come over to the booth where I was sitting.

"Sure, do you mind if I bring my girlfriend Judy with me?" she asked.

"Not at all, if you don't mind sitting with my two friends," I said.

"That'll be fine," she replied.

Darlene and Judy moved over to our booth. Jim made an uncomfortable fifth person but didn't seem to mind. He eventually got tired and went back to the barracks. The rest of the evening went by quickly. We all went to one of the all night restaurants out on the Beltway for breakfast.

CHAPTER 7

The first week, of the third training section, started with an introduction to photography and instruction on how to use the Graflex 4X5 Camera with the Polaroid Land Attachment. We were all amazed at how big and heavy those cameras were compared to the 35mm cameras most of us knew. In addition, as a "Press Camera," we were equally shocked at how difficult they appeared to be to use. The camera housing was approximately 6" x 8", and came closed up in a box effect. If you opened the front cover, it folded down and exposed a set of metal tracks. Inside the camera body was the actual camera front with its lens plate and bellows. If you slid a latch to one side, the camera body and lens plate would extend out onto the metal tracks, and the bellows would extend behind the lens plate. You then needed to lock the latch back to hold the lens plate and bellows in place. Either you could then look through the viewfinder, or you could open up the back of the camera body and expose the ground glass plate, with which you could focus through the lens. Each student was issued a Graflex Camera Kit, which came in a black hard case and included the Graflex Camera, a Polaroid back for the use of Polaroid Film, a tubular flash unit attachment and several boxes of Polaroid Film and flash bulbs. In addition, each student received a rather large, bulky and clumsy wooden tripod. We were told to practice with the camera as much as possible over the next two weeks. Most of the students had a basic knowledge of photography, but the use of a 4X5 inch format camera was new to the majority of us.

Graflex Speed Graphic Camera Photo provided by the Author

Needless to say, more than one of us got a nasty burn, from grabbing a hot flashbulb after just taking a flash picture. Those #5 bulbs were large and generated a lot of heat. The first day, we just spent our time going around certain sections of the training facility, taking photographs of anything and everything we could find from inert objects to people. Of course, Guy had to find the opportunity to sneak several photos of Sherri. The object was to just get familiar with the Graflex and how to use it. We were to take everything from large whole room photos to micro-shots of very small details such as fingerprints. The entire first week we continued to work with the cameras. We shot photos in and around the Tempo E Building and the National Mall. We took the cameras back to the barracks each night and shot photos on and around Bolling AFB. Several of us practiced taking photos of vehicle tire tread imprints in mud and dirt. We also took photos of individual tree leaves, showing the stems and veins.

On the evening of the third day, I was alone outside the barracks taking photographs. I looked up from the camera and saw Skip walking towards me.

"Jake, I'm really having trouble with this darned camera. I know we've had our differences in the past, but I really need your help. You seem to have mastered this miserable thing better than some of us. Will you please help me learn how to use it?"

"Skip, you just can't have any idea how much your plight with the camera bothers me! In fact, if I had a 'tear glass,' I would try to catch one of the tears of joy streaming down my cheek. You can go fly a kite, for all I care. I wouldn't help you for any amount of money."

"I didn't think you would hold a grudge for this long," he replied.

"Well, now you know. I sincerely hope you fail the test just so I can get rid of you. I don't want to have anything else to do with you."

"Fine then, I'll try to get help from someone else," he replied.

In the second week, we started learning how to "dust" and "lift" fingerprints from pieces of evidence. This was very challenging at first. After you decided where fingerprints were, that could be evidence; you first would dust for prints using talcum powder and a small Camelhair brush. The powder would make the print visible. Next, you used a special fingerprint lifting tape, or regular Scotch Tape, and placed it over the area with the fingerprint. You then lifted, or transferred, the print by pulling the tape away from the surface where the fingerprint was located.

It took a lot of practice and many mistakes, but the majority of the class did fairly well with learning the process of dusting and lifting prints. Once you got the knack of it, it wasn't all that bad. To my great satisfaction, I noticed that Skip was having as much trouble with fingerprints as he did with the camera. By the end of the third training section, most of us were getting much better at both methods of evidence collection.

To my shear enjoyment, Skip Felton failed the third examination and had to wash back to take the third section over again. It seemed he just wasn't much into learning the physical evidence collection methods. It wasn't quite the nature of a dilemma I'd hoped for him, but it would do for now. I was through with him, at least for the time being.

Even though he was still around, he was in the class behind us, and I didn't have any other trouble from him. We just continued to avoid each other.

On the morning of the first day of the fourth training section, we were given instruction on the actual collection of evidence in a crime scene. We were told what to look for as evidence and how to start taking photographs first from an overall crime-scene perspective and then narrow it down to individual pieces of evidence. Everything in a crime scene had to be photographed before it was touched and/or processed in any manner. Then each piece of evidence had to be individually photographed, properly collected and preserved and its wrapping marked as to what it was and where in the crime scene it had been found.

If there was a body in the crime scene, its location relevant to the overall scene had to be documented, as well as its condition, position and clothing (or lack thereof). Detailed photographs of each marking, physical damage, entry and exit wounds had to be taken. If there were specific blood pools, splatters, droppings or markings on any object, they had to be individually photographed in detail, and their relationship and location in regards to the body identified.

On the fifth day, the students were divided into four groups and were assigned individual crime scenes to process, with even more detailed inspections of the crime scenes to include photography and actual evidence collection. The students had received plenty of instruction on how to do it. Now we would put our newfound knowledge into practice.

I had been placed with Jim, Guy and another person named John. Guy was in charge of the investigation. According to the information we had been provided, our crime scene was a robbery. The robbery had been found at 6:00 am on a Monday morning. Our crime scene was a replica of a robbery of an overseas, on-base newspaper distribution office. We had been provided with a copy of a clipping of a "Stars & Stripes" newspaper article as our reference. We had been told that a body (a dummy) was located inside the room that was to be our crime scene.

'Stars and Stripes' manager found dead in office Mon.

Pacific "Stars and Stripes" District Manager Oscar K. Cabrera was found dead of gunshot wounds Monday morning in his office here by an employe of the bureau. As of Tuesday afternoon, agents of the Philippine Constabulary and the Air Force Office of Special Investigations could find no weapon and reported there were no suspects.

USAF Hospital Clark spokesmen said the 50-year-old Filipino was pronounced dead at 10:15 a.m. Monday.

Mr. Cabrera is survived by his wife, Trinidad, his parents and seven children.

An investigation by the Philippine Constabulary and the Air Force Office of Special Investigations was initiated immediately and is still in progress.

Copy of "Stars & Stripes Article," provided by Author

"Alright, guys, everyone put on your gloves, and let's get started," said Guy. "Jim, I want you to make the sketch of the crime scene."

"John, I want you to take the photos of the crime scene."

"Jake, you and I will start at the entry door and dust for fingerprints. We will lift and preserve any we may find."

"After we are through looking at the entry door area, we will then examine the body and look for any evidence around it."

"Guy, if you'll just give me a few minutes to make some preliminary notes of the entrance and layout of the room, John can then start his photos. Is that OK?" asked Jim.

"Sure thing Jim."

"John, you can start the photos from outside the entry door. Then work your way into the room and around, starting from right to left, since that is where the body is located."

"After Jim gets his initial notes, and you get the photos up to and including the body as it is, Jake and I will start the examination of the body. You can continue taking photos of the body as we examine and move it."

"Sounds good," John, said.

After Jim made his initial notes of the entry area and door, which did not appear to have been forced, and the location and position of the body, he moved on into the room. John followed closely behind Jim taking photos of the entryway, the door, its door handle and lock, and then the location and position of the body.

"Guy, there are two good fingerprints and some smudged ones on the outside doorknob," I said as I finished dusting the knob.

"Good, let me lift them before we do anything else," said Guy.

I then dusted the inside door knob and lock and got four good fingerprints, which Guy proceeded to lift. The initial review of the good lifted fingerprints indicated the prints on the outside of the door were different from those on the inside of the door.

"It looks to me like the victim had opened the door with his right hand, with the right side of his body facing the door opening, from the way he is laying," I said.

"Yes, I agree with that," said Guy. "Apparently, whoever robbed him shot him as soon as he opened the door."

"Jim and John, are you through with what you need at this point, so Jake and I can start looking at the victim?" asked Guy.

"Sure, boss," they both said at the same time.

"Jake, look at this, there appears to be a bullet wound on the victim's left side. How could that have happened if he was standing with his right side facing the door opening?"

"It doesn't make any sense, Guy."

After further examination, we discovered there was a coin in his right shirt pocket, and it had been hit with something.

"I'll be darned, I think the bullet hit the coin and ricocheted through his body and out his left side. This man was probably dead before he hit the ground," I stated.

"Then that is why there is blood around his left side, but what about the blood around his head?" asked Guy.

"Look, there is a wound in the back of his head," I said. "That hole looks too small to be an exit wound."

"Where is the exit wound then?" asked Guy. "Could the bullet have stayed inside his head?"

"I wouldn't think so," I replied.

As I looked closely at the victim's face, there was no evidence of an exit wound. I opened the left eyelid first and observed his eye. When I opened the right eyelid, all I saw was mush.

"Darn," I stated. "The bullet actually exited through the left eyelid with no exit wound visible at all!"

"I guess that since the bullet only hit soft matter and no bone, it didn't create a large exit wound," Guy said out loud.

As we looked around the body and the immediate vicinity, we found a badly deformed bullet lying under a nearby table. We stopped Jim and John so they could include the bullet location in their sketch and photos.

As Guy picked up the bullet he said, "It is a small caliber probably a .32."

We lifted all of the fingerprints from the body so we could compare them to the prints found on the inside doorknob.

We finished all of our crime scene investigation, sketch, photos and evidence collection.

Our conclusion we handed in, along with our evidence, was that the man had in fact been shot pointblank as soon as he opened the door. He had somehow fallen and ended up on his stomach with his face pointing down to the floor. As we surmised, he had been shot in the right side, and the bullet had ricocheted off the coin and traveled through his body. He had very probably been dead by the time he hit the floor. Whoever shot him had put a *coup de grâce* shot through his head from the rear. The bullet, being a small .32 caliber, had literally cut through his left eyelid, without any visible exit wound.

"That was an excellent crime scene investigation and evidence collection." Captain Dawson stated.

"Thank you, sir," replied Guy. "I feel my team did a great job of working together."

All students in the class completed the fourth examination and were going to start the fifth and final training section, except for the three who failed.

CHAPTER 8

On Monday morning, of the fifth and final two-week section of the OSI School, Captain Dawson started the day off with a surprise quiz.

"This is just to give me an idea of where we may need to concentrate regarding your knowledge of handling sources, surveillance techniques and executive protection," Dawson said.

Most of the class did fair on the quiz, and it gave us some perspective on what we would need to learn in the next two weeks.

We spent the first three days reviewing the basics of vetting and handling sources. It was made perfectly clear – any investigative and/or intelligence operation would be highly dependent upon obtaining good source information on a timely basis. Dawson went over where good sources could be found on a military base and the type of personnel that we should be looking for. He spoke of how we should always be on the lookout for anyone who might be willing to work with us as a source. He also spoke of how to always be thinking about whom we might be able to use as a source, if they had been on the wrong side of the law.

The last two days of the first week were spent learning the basics of proper surveillance techniques. We were shown movies of surveillance operations, which were used to graphically introduce us to ways a surveillance should be conducted. We were also introduced to executive protection operations, since a large portion of those types of operations relied upon good surveillance techniques.

During the final week of our training, we spent two days out on the streets of Washington, D.C. in civilian clothes, conducting practical surveillance operations. We were excited about being out of our Air Force Uniforms and in coats and ties, which we would wear after we became special agents. Again, we were divided into three five-person groups and one four-person group. Each group had radios with concealable earpieces for communication between group members. We were advised to carry extra shirts, hats and jackets so we could change our looks if we thought we had been "made," or had been identified as being part of the surveillance team.

I was chosen as one of the group leaders and was allowed to pick my five-person team. I chose Jim Connel, George Carriby, Guy Purvis and one of the regular agents in the class named Richard Trent. He was a down-to-earth type person my friends and I had gotten to know. I chose Richard as he had done very well throughout the school and he was non-descript with no outstanding physical attributes, so I felt he would be able to blend in with a crowd and not be noticed. Although I hadn't spent much time with Richard, I knew he came from upstate New York and seemed to have a good head on his shoulders. In addition, he appeared to have a good sense of humor, so I figured he would fit in with our group. Unfortunately, with George and his size, I knew I was taking a chance with him as a team member, but what he gave up in size he made up for with his quick thinking and determination. Besides, with that Texas drawl of his, he could confuse just about anyone as they probably wouldn't understand him, and that might come in handy.

The "rabbit," or the person to be surveilled, we were given to follow turned out to be a female. We were given a photo of her for each of our team members. Our instructions were simple: follow her where ever she went in downtown Washington, D.C., make notes as to what she did and if she attempted to contact anyone in any way and try not to let the rabbit "burn," or make, you. We were told that our rabbit would leave the northwest corner of the Tempo E Building, at exactly 1:00 pm. She had been instructed to walk towards the new J. Edgar Hoover FBI Building that was being built between Ninth and Tenth Streets on the north side of Pennsylvania Avenue. She would be wearing blue jeans with a white blouse and a light beige jacket.

I got my team together in the cafeteria for a briefing while we ate lunch. We were all excited about the prospects of the afternoon surveillance and wanted to make it go as well as possible. My plan was to have four of my team members outside of Tempo E at various locations within line-of-sight of the northwest corner of the building. The fifth member of the team would be standing in an office, just inside the northwest corner of the building, and would have a view of anyone exiting the building at that location. Our objective was to pick up our rabbit as she left the building, with as little chance of her seeing any of us as possible.

"OK," I asked, "who wants to be in the office to let us know exactly when the rabbit leaves the building?"

"I'll take that position," said Jim.

"Fine, George, I want you to be located at the northeast end of the main Smithsonian Institution Building. You should be able to find a spot that will allow you to see her as she leaves the building. You'll be far enough away that she shouldn't be able to identify you as part of the surveillance team."

"Guy, I want you to be located at the west side of the front entrance of the National Gallery of Art. I figure that, out of all of us, you should be perfectly comfortable with that location, seeing as how you've been there recently!"

Immediately, Jim, George and I all snickered at the same time.

"What's that all about?" asked Richard.

"Never mind, it's a private joke," I replied.

"Richard, you and I will be standing at the bronze Triceratops Dinosaur, which is located in front of the National Museum of Natural History."

"We should all be able to have the rabbit in view the moment she leaves Tempo E, and Jim will notify us by radio that she's departed the building. Each of us should allow her to cross the National Mall before we start to follow her. We'll all have her in view and will be able to ID her long before she even starts to see anyone following her. Jim will be last to start moving, as she'll be expecting someone to follow her out of the building. Jim, when you see her reach the other side of the Mall, you should exit the building and walk towards where George was located. I want all of us to give her plenty of room for the first part of the surveillance, as I'm sure we'll have to be in close to her as the afternoon wears on."

"Use your radios to keep in touch with team members and to keep up with the rabbit's location. However, be sure to keep your earpieces out of sight, if possible. Are there any questions? No, OK then, finish lunch and get into position. It is 12:45 pm."

At exactly 1:00 pm, our rabbit exited the northwest corner of Tempo E and headed directly across the National Mall towards Ninth Street and Constitution Avenue. As planned, all of my team members allowed her to get well on her way before we moved at all. As our rabbit passed the southeast corner of the National Museum of Natural History Building and headed north on Ninth Street, Richard started walking about a half of a block behind her. I blended in with some tourists and followed on the same side of the street about a block back. Guy, again in with some people, had started moving towards her as she approached the Natural History Building, and he ended up on the opposite side of Ninth from her and about a half a block back. Jim and George remained back about one block and were told to exchange places with Richard and Guy as soon as the rabbit crossed Pennsylvania Avenue.

The only thing visible, for the new J. Edgar Hoover FBI Building, at that time, was a block square monster excavation in the ground. There was, of course, plywood fencing all around the block with observation holes where a person could stand and watch the construction men and equipment working in the hole. That provided an excellent chance for our rabbit to stop, to feign watching the construction but instead to have a perfect chance to try to burn anyone who might have been following her.

Luckily, Jim had crossed Ninth prior to Constitution Avenue, which put him across the street from the rabbit and George.

Photo of the early construction of the J. Edgar Hoover Building.
Courtesy of the Federal Bureau of Investigation

I immediately radioed George and told him to turn left onto Constitution to escape having to walk by the rabbit. At that time, I came up Ninth Street, crossed Constitution and proceeded to pass the rabbit and stop at a viewing hole up at the end of the block. That put me in front of the rabbit, Guy across Ninth on the other side of the street, George around the corner and out of view of the rabbit, and Richard and Jim about a half of a block behind us and on the south side of Constitution Avenue.

After what seemed to be an eternity, the rabbit looked around her in all directions and then started walking north again on Ninth. Richard and Jim crossed Constitution and were walking together, north on Ninth. At the corner of Ninth and E Street, the rabbit crossed the intersection, crossed E Street and entered a multistory department store. I radioed Richard to catch up and for him and Guy to follow the rabbit into the store. They were instructed to make mental notes as to what the rabbit did in the store and what she looked at. As it turned out, the rabbit went directly to the women's clothing department and lingered there for a while looking at clothes. Richard and Guy were comfortable in the store and managed to shop within eyesight of the rabbit. They got a list of most of what she looked at.

After the rabbit departed the department store, she crossed Ninth Street again and walked west down E Street. I had managed to change my shirt and hat before she came out of the department store and was looking in the recessed entryway of a shoe store on E Street when she passed me. I let her get half way down the block and then started following her. George and Jim were across E Street looking in a couple of the observation holes at the nonexistent FBI Building. At the corner of E Street and Tenth Street, the rabbit crossed Tenth and then crossed E Street and entered a bar that was located directly on the corner. Since I was closest to her, I radioed the team to take up positions accordingly, and I would follow her into the bar. I would be out of radio contact for a few minutes, as I was going to remove my radio earpiece as I entered the bar so the rabbit would not see it.

As I entered the bar, I saw there were tables in the front section of the room and a long row of booths, along the E Street side of the building. I immediately noticed the rabbit was sitting alone in a booth about half way down the wall. I didn't see an obvious rear door, so I figured that wouldn't be an option for her. I walked over to a booth near the front of the room that was located directly across from the men's and women's restrooms.

I saw the rabbit was having some type of a drink, so when the waitress asked me what I wanted, I asked for a Budweiser. There was a TV playing behind the bar, so I pretended to watch it and not be too interested in what else was happening in the room.

After ten to fifteen minutes, the rabbit got out of her booth and went to the women's restroom. I remained seated and finished my beer. Shortly after she entered the restroom, she came back out, turned to the right and left the bar. I notified the team that she was moving again so they could pick her up as she exited the building.

As soon as she had left the bar, I called the waitress over to my booth.

"I'm on a surveillance, and I'm following the lady that just departed the bar. Can you please tell me what the lady had ordered to drink?"

The waitress replied, "It was a Vodka Collins."

"I need another favor please. Can you go into the women's restroom to see if the lady left anything there?"

When the waitress came back she said, "I didn't see anything the lady may have left in the restroom."

I slipped her a couple of dollars, said, "Thank you very much," and departed the bar.

The remainder of the afternoon went about the same as the earlier part had gone. The rabbit walked a few more blocks around D.C., entered another store and then made her way back to the Tempo E Building. My team followed her at a safe distance and made notes of anything she did. We all got back to Tempo E a few minutes after the rabbit did and entered through different entrances. We went back to our classroom to determine what we were to do next. Our three instructors were there, as were a couple of the other surveillance teams.

"Well, Jake, how'd you think your team's surveillance went?" asked Captain Dawson.

"I think we did very well, sir," I replied. "I think we have a very detailed list of our rabbit's directions, actions and activities."

"OK then, bring your team, and we'll go to meet your rabbit."

We went downstairs to a small room. When we entered the room, our rabbit was sitting there waiting for us.

"Jake Douglas, meet Laurie Brownfeld. Laurie, this is Jake Douglas. He was the leader of the surveillance team that followed you this afternoon. The other team members here are Jim Connel, George Carriby, Guy Purvis and Richard Trent. Laurie is a secretary upstairs in the Criminal Investigations Directorate."

"Good afternoon, Laurie, I feel I already know you," I said with a slight grin.

"Good afternoon, Jake," she said. "Other than the fact I can now place you in a couple of different locations in D.C. and the bar, where we both enjoyed a cool drink on a hot afternoon, I must admit that I certainly did not place you as a surveillant today."

"I'm glad to hear that," I replied, with a sigh of relief.

"I do admit, however, that I had picked George as a possible surveillance team member out there on the streets, as he got way too close to me at the new FBI Building, and he would be hard to miss anywhere. However, I did not place Jim, Guy or Richard as team members even though I now recall seeing two of them in the first department store I entered. I would say that, as a team, you all did very well."

"I think you did a great job of leading us around town," I said. "And I did find out from the waitress at the bar that you had a Vodka Collins to drink, and you did not leave anything in the women's restroom."

"Excellent," said Captain Dawson. "Laurie has been a rabbit for our training classes for three or four times now, so the fact she didn't burn all of your team members, I would say speaks highly for your techniques."

The entire class was relieved the surveillance exercise was over. The remainder of our last week of school went by quickly. We took our final examination on Wednesday of that week. I completed the final exam with an average of 84.7 for the course. On Thursday, June 26, 1969, the remaining nineteen members of Dawson's Dogs each received their graduation certificate from the OSI Commander, Brigadier General William K. Raduci. We were now special agents in the Air Force Office of Special Investigations!

CHAPTER 9

On September 1, 1969, George, Jim, Guy and I all started our Technical Agents Training School. Much to my dismay, Skip Felton was also there as he had graduated in the class behind us. We were back in a training situation for another six weeks. This time, things were a little different though, as we four friends now lived in the area and were stationed at OSI District 4, located in Suitland Hall, Maryland. Suitland Hall was only a few miles outside of D.C. and just a little ways from Andrews Air Force Base, Maryland. Another technical agent had been assigned to District 4 after us, and he was Tom Mostello. Skip had been stationed at OSI District 13 in Omaha, Nebraska. There were a couple of other OSI technical agents in this class with us, who had also graduated from the basic school after us. We met Jim Haug and Charles Keio. They were also assigned to District 13. So, once again, I was thrown in with my antagonist. We managed to keep out of each other's way.

The first week of our tech school proved to be extremely difficult, as believe it or not, our instructor, "The Professor," actually spoke in mathematics almost exclusively. He ended up about halfway through the first morning with a complete blackboard full of mind-numbing mathematical formulas! I was completely befuddled and certain I had somehow taken a wrong turn somewhere and was in the wrong class. I looked around the classroom at that point to see if I was the only one with that dumb, lost look on my face. To my relief, all but a couple of people in the class had the same look. Tom Mostello seemed to know what was going on, as well as Charles Keio.

The school did not improve until after the third day. By then, I was ready to transfer to being a regular agent.

After the third day, the instructor starting speaking in what I recognized as English. Much to our surprise, we found out "The Professor" had been teaching us about radio wave propagation and transmitter and receiver theory. And – we thought we already knew that stuff.

It actually got very interesting after that, and our instructor changed to a man who referred to himself as "Doc." We started learning about telephone systems, components, wiring and instruments. We had to learn about the complete systems so we could analyze them to determine if they'd been modified or changed surreptitiously. We also needed to know how they worked so we could test them to be sure they did not contain any clandestine surveillance devices. Next, we studied the fundamentals of intercom systems for the same reasons. Finally, we got into the types of microphones and speakers and how to test them for operational functions.

When we actually started learning the basics of a technical surveillance survey, we were taught the two basic sections of a survey were the non-alerting phase and the alerting phase. The objective of the non-alerting phase is to attempt to determine if an area contains any sort of a clandestine radio frequency (RF) or video transmitting system without alerting the opposition that a survey is being conducted. Once the first phase is completed, then the alerting phase is conducted in an attempt to find any type of surveillance device that may be in the area but may be turned off or no longer working.

It's called the alerting phase because the team physically looks into each item and area that can be opened, moved, looked in, under or above.

Obviously, that type of activity can get a little loud.

During four more weeks of learning how and where to look for clandestine surveillance devices, we also were taught where and how to put in a clandestine surveillance device. The theory being, that if you knew where and how to put in a surveillance device you would also know where and how to look for them.

All of us technical agents took to the new training and experiences like ducks to water. Our background in electronic maintenance and the theory of radio communications paid off well for us. And, although we learned a lot during the six-week technical school, we were told we would continue to learn the "business" for quite some time in an on-the-job format.

After a total of six weeks, on October 10, 1969, we once again graduated from an OSI school and were fully trained OSI technical agents, aka: Hobbyshop Boys.

Skip returned to his new assignment, and he and I only crossed paths on rare occasions after that.

After the five new technical agents returned to District 4, we were all placed under the watchful eye of a fully qualified technical agent at Suitland Hall and assigned to teams. I was assigned to work with one Ed Linz as my trainer. I didn't know it at first, but Ed and I were to establish a close friendship that would last to this day.

PART II

THE OPERATIONS

OPERATION I: THE BLACK MARKET PROFITEERS
Sub-Operation: The Money Thefts

Location: Guam, U.S. Territory

Main Allegation: Black Marketing of BX Items in South East Asia
Second Allegation: Theft of Money from
Vending Machines –Guam

CHAPTER 1

O ur duties for the first couple of years we were at OSI District 4 were primarily restricted to learning the ins and outs of technical surveillance countermeasures (TSCM) work. At that time, District 4 was one of the largest Technical Services Districts in the entire organization. It covered from North Carolina to Maine and from the East Coast to Ohio. We did a lot of traveling, and I certainly saw a lot of the United States I had never been to. Our primary work though was over at the Pentagon. We spent a lot of time there. We also learned, quickly, not to allow Jim Connel to get his hands on the keys of any government vehicle we used. It was a lesson that took a couple of times for us to learn but, after that, on days we were going to drive somewhere and the possibility existed Connel would be going, Jim Mostello would get the keys to the vehicle the first thing in the morning so Connel would not have the opportunity. Connel wasn't necessarily a bad driver, although there were certainly people who would argue with that. It was just that while he was driving he wanted to be a part of any conversation that might be occurring in the car. So, he would be driving along and talking and as we would be passing an exit we needed to take he would say, "Oh, I guess I was supposed to get off there," as he watched the exit go bye! So, then we would spend the next thirty minutes trying to get back to where we were supposed to be. However, bless his pointed little head; he was sure a good worker.

Another thing that happened to all of the technical agents in about 1971 was the Air Force came to OSI and said there were radio maintenance personnel who were going back to Vietnam for the second time. The Air Force wanted to start taking some of the OSI technical services agents and returning them to duty in the regular Air Force. Of course, after OSI had taken the time to train the technical agents, they were not interested in letting us go back to our former radio maintenance jobs in the Air Force. Therefore, OSI forced all of the technical agents to cross-train to the same career field as the OSI regular agents. That meant we all had to take correspondence courses and then test to obtain the other career field designation.

One day, after I had been at District 4 for two and a half years, I was told to report to Major Point's office. It was January 1972. This was not a normal request, so I was somewhat concerned about why I was being summoned to the TSD chief's office. As I stood outside the solid wooden door, I gathered my composure and searched my mind for anything I could recall which might have happened recently causing me to be in trouble.

My mind raced back to the time when, as a gesture of friendly humor, I had called our former TSD chief, Maj. Keith Fitchinsen, "shorty." He was about six foot 4 inches tall. Seeing as how I was a lowly staff sergeant at the time and calling an officer anything but sir was considered a form of fraternization, the major informed Ed Linz of my transgression. Needless to say, I was chewed out by Ed Linz!

Nothing came to mind, so I struck the door with the customary two hard knocks and waited for the responding voice of Maj. Point telling me to enter.

"Come in," I heard the distinct voice of Maj. Point call out.

As I entered the room, I was surprised to see my friend Ed Linz along with Lt. Colonel Richard O'Leary, the director of technical services, and his second in command, Major John Hanson.

Darn, I thought to myself and almost blurted it out. *What the heck have I done now?*

The look on my face must have given me away, as Maj. Point immediately said, "Relax, Jake, you're not in trouble."

Linz just looked up at me and grinned that big crap-eating grin I knew so well. Linz was getting a big bang out of my obvious discomfort.

Maj. Point said, "Sit down, Jake. You know Col. O'Leary and Maj. Hanson don't you?"

"Yes, sir, we've met."

I always felt uncomfortable around Maj. Hanson for some reason. I often thought that Hanson had it out for anyone who had been in Capt. Dawson's Basic Class in 1969, as that was when OSI School Director's Secretary Sherri Green had changed her personality. Hanson had been stationed at the OSI Headquarters at the time and had been a good friend of Sherri's. I'd overheard him on at least one occasion mention to someone he was sure something had happened in the spring of 1969 that changed Sherri and her character, as she just wasn't the same after that. Of course, I was relatively sure he had no idea about Sherri and Guy. Otherwise, Guy would have been kicked out of OSI.

Maj. Point motioned to Col. O'Leary and said, "Go ahead, sir."

O'Leary cleared his throat and spoke in his fatherly voice. "Jake, we have an important case we've done a lot of preliminary work on, and we need someone new to run it in the field.

Ordinarily, we would use one of our more experienced people for an operation such as this, but they're all either busy or have already been involved in this operation, and we can't take the chance of re-exposing them to the Subject of the investigation. Ed Linz and Maj. Point, based upon your performance in the outfit to date, have recommended you. Are you available for a possible lengthy trip to Guam?"

I didn't hesitate, "Yes, sir."

I knew that to be a case manager for a field case, let alone an important one such as this one, was every newbie's dream. Although I was not a certified newbie, I had not been around very long and didn't know if I had really proven myself yet.

As was the case at that time in technical services, a new tech agent only was chosen for a technical support operation when everyone else, who was a regular support operations person, was busy on another job. If you were picked and did well, then you were considered to be a regular support operations person. Screw it up and, well, it would probably be a long time before you got another chance.

I knew my rise in the organization was directly attributable to my association and friendship with Ed Linz. He had taken a liking to me right off and had taken me under his wing from the start.

My handling of our bread and butter work, TSCM cases, and the special training of U.S. Air Force military *attachés* I had participated in had won me a lot of respect, and Ed had gone out of his way to publicize my work within the organization.

Everyone in the organization knew Ed. He had the reputation of being somewhat arrogant and cocky. He's the person who obviously is in charge (of everything) and has no hesitation about letting everyone know it. At 6', he's of a thin build but is an imposing figure, at least in his speech and actions. He had a habit of using a little too much hair oil and combing his hair straight back. It didn't take me long to hang him with the nickname "Slick." Unfortunately, for him, that moniker was picked-up by most people who knew him well. In his mind, he was the OSI! In addition, because of his way with women, to a select few, he was known as "Superman." However, do not take me wrong, Ed certainly knew his electronics and investigative business. That's why he was one of the better trainers in OSI. He was usually involved in the biggest and best cases and seemed to be the go-to guy when a particularly tough investigation came up.

"Maj. Hanson, would you please brief Maj. Point and Jake?" asked O'Leary.

"Sure thing, sir," replied Hanson in his deep raspy voice.

"Well, gentlemen, we have a very reliable source who has told us of a major black market operation, involving the military exchange system, primarily on Air Force bases in Southeast Asia area during the Vietnam War.

"We're talking about tens of millions of dollars the Subject of the investigation has made by diverting multiple types of merchandise and selling it on the black market. As you know, this type of operation, besides being illegal with our Status of Forces

Agreement, always diverts many needed items that should be available to our own military personnel and civilians. Our source worked for the Subject of the investigation during most of the time the black marketing took place.

"The source is well motivated and has contacted the Internal Revenue Service and offered to work with them to catch the Subject. The source stands to possibly get as much as ten percent of any amount of income the Subject has made on the black market sales and has not claimed for tax purposes. Of course, the IRS has to prove the Subject made income that he didn't claim. It is the hopes of the IRS that the source can help prove the Subject's involvement in the black market operation."

"Wow that is some motivation!" I exclaimed. "But what has Guam got to do with the case, sir?"

"That's where the source now lives. Our source stated he has met the Subject several times on Guam, during their black market operations. It was just a convenient place to meet, and a precedent had already been set for meeting there. The initial operation plan calls for the source to attempt to get Subject to meet him on Guam. What we want you to do, Jake, is to record any conversations that might occur between the source and Subject. You'll have to travel to Guam and reconnoiter all of the major hotel bars and restaurants on the island where the source and Subject could possibly meet."

"Darn, that'll be hard work. Is OSI going to pay for my bar and restaurant bills?" I asked.

I immediately got a deep frown from Maj. Point, a grin from Ed and Col. O'Leary and a deeper frown from Maj. Hanson.

"Sorry, gentlemen, I got carried away."

"Your travel to Guam will be soon, so you can complete any necessary reconnoitering, get totally familiar with the island, make contact with the U.S. Immigration & Customs personnel at the Guam International Airport, and become familiar with the airport layout, parking areas and the Northwest Airlines services and flight arrival times," Hanson continued. "We plan to keep you away from any public contact with the source. Your only physical contact with him will be at the Naval Hospital Marianas Facility or on Anderson Air Force Base (AAFB). Otherwise, you'll only talk to him by telephone, and that'll be as limited as possible to prevent any possible compromise of the case. We've no idea if Subject has any personal friends or potential accomplices' on Guam."

"Is there any plan on how I'm to record the possible conversations?" I asked.

"No, that'll be for you to plan and for Ed to get the approval," stated Col. O'Leary.

"Any preconceived ideas at all? Or am I completely on my own to assess the situation and come up with possible ways to record any conversations?"

"We have faith in you and your assessment of the situation when you get the chance to evaluate the conditions on Guam."

Besides, I'll be holding a tight leash on you and, as you can see, there'll be fairly strict observation from the top," advised Ed Linz.

"This one is basically up to you to call as you see it and as Ed can get approval for," said Maj. Hanson. "When do you want to leave for Guam?"

"I certainly appreciate your faith in me, and I'll do everything in my power to make this operation happen with the best results possible," I said. "It'll take me three or four days to review equipment and decide what I think I'll need."

"Just keep in touch with Ed and let us know your plans," said Hanson.

Everyone shook hands, and the meeting adjourned.

I caught Ed on the way out of the room and whispered, "Thanks, ol' buddy, I owe you one!"

I spent the next day collecting all of the information I could find about the island of Guam, its international airport, the location of its major hotels, the type and location of U.S. military installations, roads and highways, towns and services.

I also made contact with the officials in the U.S. Immigrations and Customs Service Office in Washington, D.C. I wanted to have them notify their office at the airport on Guam of my arrival and request their assistance.

I also found out as much as possible about the source, his work location, home location, telephone numbers and his normal habits, hobbies, entertainment and nightlife. I also needed to know where source and Subject had typically met in the past.

On the second day, I had our Office Secretary Julie Healer make airline reservations for me.

She was very efficient, and always enjoyed setting up travel arrangements for the men in the office. I would be traveling on regular commercial flights and would arrive on Guam at 1:00 pm, on a Sunday. That meant leaving D.C. on Saturday evening. Julie also arranged for me to stay on base at Anderson AFB. I would have three days, after arriving on Guam, to reconnoiter the hotels and do all of the other preliminary activities I needed to do. At that point, I had to have my initial operations plan completed and ready to submit to Ed Linz for the approval process.

During the long hours of the flights from Washington, D.C. to Guam, I had nothing better to do than just sit and watch the aircraft punching holes in the sky. Therefore, I had plenty of time to think about how I might be able to "wire," or conceal a device on, the source to overhear any conversations between him and Subject. I could not consider wiring a room or car, since there was a slim possibility that is where the two would meet. They were more than likely going to meet in a very public place. I had little choice but to wire the source himself or have him carry something to conceal the bug in.

CHAPTER 2

I arrived at the Guam International Airport, with its mushroom looking entrance pillars, on Sunday. I wanted to check on airline arrival times so I went to the Northwest Airlines Ticketing Counter.

"Pardon me," I said to the ticketing agent on duty, whose nametag said Tony. "Can you please tell me when your normal flights from the U.S. mainland arrive on Guam?"

"There're only two flights a day coming into Guam from the mainland," Tony replied. "One arrives at 1:00 pm, and the other one arrives at 11:30 pm."

"Is that every day of the week?" I asked.

"Yes, that's all we have."

Since I was in the airport, I also checked in with the Immigration and Customs Office. I wanted to establish my credentials with them so I would be able to make telephonic contact each day to determine if my Subject had arrived on one of the Northwest Airlines flights.

As I opened the door into the Immigration and Customs Office, I observed a nice looking woman with red hair and a pretty face standing behind the counter. As I entered, she looked up and smiled.

"Excuse me, Miss," I said. "My name is Jake Douglass, and I work with the Air Force Office of Special Investigations. Is your supervisor here?

"I'm Heather Lockran and I'm the shift supervisor. Can I help you?"

"Yes, I was wondering if you received notice from your headquarters in Washington, D.C. about my arrival."

"Yes, we've been expecting you. I understand you will be calling us daily after the arrival of each Northwest Airlines flights and will be asking if a particular person had arrived on the flight. Is that correct?"

"Yes, that's what I need to know. I will be looking for a Mr. Samuel Moore. I'd appreciate it if this information was kept just between you and any other supervisor on duty, as this is a very sensitive investigation."

"That'll not be a problem," Heather replied. "Although it'll involve myself and three other people, as we are talking two flights a day, seven days a week, and the flights are so far apart. I assure you only four people will know the name of the person you are looking for, and all of us know the importance of something like this. And by the way, you may call me Heather."

"Great. Thanks, Heather. What's the telephone number I should call?"

She gave me the number to call and told me the best times to call each day.

That afternoon, after I picked up a rental car at the airport, I drove Guam Highway One out to Anderson AFB. It was a beautiful drive, with some of it along the coast and the rest of it through lush tropical vegetation and forest. It was a typical dry season day on Guam with temperatures in the 80's.

After arriving on Anderson, I checked into the Visiting Officers Quarters (VOQ) on base.

Then I called the local OSI Detachment Commander, Captain Shaun Byer to let him know I had arrived and had checked in on base. Capt. Byer had already been advised of my pending arrival and only knew a little about the operation. I was to brief him after I arrived, and he would set up any support I might need for the operation.

"Can I come by your office in the morning to brief you on the operation?" I asked.

"Sure thing," he said. "I have a command briefing each Monday morning at 0830. How about being at my office at, say, 0945?"

"Sounds good to me," I said. "Where's your office located?"

"It's in a stand-alone, single-story building located on the right, just two blocks straight down the street from the VOQ, towards the flight line."

"I'll see you in the morning, sir."

I was sitting in the OSI Office, having coffee at 0945 when Capt. Byer got back from his command briefing.

"Well, I see that Ed Linz was correct in his description of you," said Byer. "He said you're efficient and that I would enjoy working with you."

"Thank you, sir," I replied.

"You can stop with the formalities here on the island, Jake, and just call me Shaun."

"Great, thank you, as that's always so much easier."

I provided Shaun with a full briefing on the case, what I was here to accomplish and how I intended to do it. I also offered to provide any assistance to his office and staff that might be needed while I was on Anderson.

"Funny you should mention that," he stated. I have a little theft case going currently. I just might be able to use someone with your talents."

"Oh, what would that be?" I asked.

"Well, the officer in charge of the base community center has approached me and stated he's very sure he's losing some money from his vending machines. He has noticed in the past six months the revenue collected from the vending machines has gone down, but the use of the machines does not appear to have changed. He has an assistant who is responsible for the operation of the vending machines and the collection of monies. He believes that person has started taking part of the monies collected each day but has no way to prove it."

"What'd you have in mind for me?" I asked.

"Well, I asked Ed if you're lock trained and, if so, could I use you to open the vending machines in the community center one Sunday night and make a count of the monies contained in each machine. I figure a Sunday night would be best, as that would give a whole weekend of use for the machines, so they should have plenty of coins in them. In addition, there isn't much activity on base on Sunday nights. Do you think you could do that?" Shaun asked.

"That ought to be a piece of cake," I replied, "And, yes, I always carry at least some of my lock picks with me. When would you want to have this done? I ask because, of course, I'll have to fit it into my present schedule and get an approval from Ed for the operation."

"We should be able to set it up just about any time you can be available. I'll have Lieutenant Mac Bockron open the community center for you on the night we set this thing up. Then, you can work at your leisure to pick the locks on the vending machines, count and record the monies in each machine, close everything up and leave. The next morning, you can give us the individual money counts from each machine, and then Lt. Bockron will receive the monies from his assistant and verify if any monies are missing. If so, we can arrest the assistant at that time."

"Sounds like a simple and short operation. I'll write up a quick operations plan and send it to Ed for approval, so we will be ready to go when the time is right. Can I use your secure fax to send the plan to Ed?"

"Yes, of course," replied Shaun.

Within a short time, I had completed the necessary operations plan and faxed it to Ed.

After sending the request for the lock pick operation, I told Shaun, "OK, now I better get on to my primary purpose for being here."

With a possible choice of at least five major hotels on the island, I would have no possible way of knowing in advance, where the meeting might occur. It might be remotely possible for the source to steer the meeting to a predetermined location; however, with the reported weariness of the Subject, that would be extremely difficult to do.

Early Monday afternoon, I called my source, Larry Owens, who was a real estate agent. "Larry, this is Jake Douglas. I was wondering if we could get together this afternoon to take a look at some property."

"Sure, Jake, what'd you have in mind?"

"Well, I'd like to look at some one bedroom apartments if you have any for sale."

"Great, Jake, what time and where would you like to meet?"

"How about 2:30 pm, at the gas station in Tamuning? I'll be driving a blue VW," I said.

"Fine, I'll see you then."

When I met Larry, I told him I was the OSI agent that had been sent to record any possible conversations between him and Mr. Moore.

"I'm sorry for the little white lie I used to get you here today, but I didn't want to take any chances of compromising the operation."

"That's quite alright," he replied. "I've been wondering when someone would be getting in touch with me. I thought maybe the IRS had been shining me on."

"Could you possibly come out to Anderson AFB this afternoon so we can meet in private and discuss the operation?"

"Sure, do you want to go in my car in case anyone might be watching us?" he asked.

"Good idea," I said.

As we drove out to Anderson, Larry and I passed time with small talk. Larry filled me in on Guamanian customs, a short history of the island, the typical weather patterns and some of the nice places to visit on the island.

Once we got to a safe location on Anderson, I asked Larry, "How have your meetings with Mr. Moore been arranged in the past?"

"He's always just called me out of the blue and advised he would be here in two to four days. I never had much advance notice, and we would normally meet wherever he decided, which was usually in the hotel where he stayed at the time. Normally, we would meet in an outside pool or bar area or sometimes in a dining room. It was always off by ourselves where he could see everyone around us. It was never in his room, as he didn't trust hotel rooms to be private enough."

"Ok, that's kind of what I expected," I replied. "Has he ever frisked you or appeared to be overly cautious of what you wore or carried with you?"

"No, he never frisked me, and I don't recall him being interested in what I've been wearing or carrying at the time. Being a real estate agent, I'm always carrying a briefcase and/or papers."

"Good" I replied. "That will help us in our planning. Would you be nervous carrying a recorder or transmitting device so we can record your conversation with Moore?"

"Gee, I don't know. I have never done anything like that. I think it would probably bother me, as I might be overly conscious of what I might be carrying. Therefore, I might give it away. He's very nervous about things like that."

"Well, what if we break your arm and put it in a cast?" I asked.

"*What?* You – you're kidding, *right?*"

"I'm sorry. I didn't mean we would really break your arm. What I meant to say was what if we put your arm in a cast with an ultra-small audio recorder inside the cast, and you tell everyone you broke your arm," I replied.

"Can you do that? Put a small enough recorder inside a cast, and it'd not be noticeable?"

"Well, I haven't actually done that before, but the recorder is small enough I think we could do it, and no one would be able to tell it was there. We would have to place the recorder in such a position so you could get to it easily enough to turn it on and off. What'd you say to that?"

At first Larry wasn't very happy about this idea as the tropical weather on Guam would make wearing a cast very uncomfortable. However, after much discussion, he agreed it would be the best way to hide a bug on his body.

"I guess we could try it," Larry said.

Therefore, it was decided that when we knew the Subject was coming to Guam, Larry would have an "accident" somewhere while he was out showing a property and break his arm. Then, as a cast was put on his arm at the Navy Hospital Marianas, a Nagra SN ultra-miniature reel-to-reel tape recorder would be placed inside the cast. The Nagra recorder was approximately 5.67" x 3.98" x 1.02" in size. It used special 1/8" audiotapes mounted on special open reel spools, operating at a tape speed of 3.75 inches per second. We would fix it so the recorder could be turned on and off with the use of a pencil stuck through the opening around the palm of his hand. The Nagra used two AA size batteries that gave the recorder a battery life of approximately five hours. Therefore, even if Larry had to turn it on early, he would have plenty of time to cover a meeting.

Since Larry worked in a real estate office, he was often mobile and could easily say he had slipped on a stairway and cracked his radius bone when he fell.

Tuesday morning, I drove over to the Naval Hospital Marianas to recruit a Navy Corpsman who could handle the job of putting the cast and recorder on Larry's arm when the time came.

I was introduced to HM-1 Tad Gueyer and briefed him on exactly what I would need him to do. I was told he would be available to assist me with what I needed.

By Tuesday afternoon, I had a good operations plan laid out and ready to submit. I was making a telephone call within minutes after every Northwest aircraft landed to determine if the Subject had arrived on the latest flight. I had reconnoitered most of the better hotels on the island and had picked out the best positions to observe and record a possible meeting. I knew the route, on Highway 1, between the airport and downtown Agana, Guam. In addition, Larry and I had discussed the overall purpose for the operation, what he would be trying to get the Subject to talk about, his normal work and social habits and his feelings about doing the overall operation.

"Larry, are you sure you can be available by telephone immediately after the times the Northwest flights arrived on Guam?" I asked.

"Sure, that won't be a problem at all," he said.

"As soon as I've verified Mr. Moore has been on a flight, I'll call you and let you know of the situation."

"I'm sure that shortly after Moore arrives, he'll call me and set up a meeting time and place. I'll attempt to get him to meet me at the Hilton but, of course, I can't push too hard for that location," Larry stated.

With all of the potential aspects of the operation covered, I sent my operations plan to Ed Linz for approval on Wednesday morning. After the plan was approved, Larry would call Subject, and attempt to set up a meeting on Guam. It would take at least three to four days to get the plan approved, and then Larry had to make contact with Subject.

CHAPTER 3

Now I had some time to relax and unwind a bit. I decided to go play a round of golf. I had been told Anderson had a great course with several challenging holes. After arriving at the golf course and renting some clubs, I thought it best to hit a bucket of balls to limber up and test my swing. I walked to the driving range and saw there were only two other people there. The golf shop pro had told me it was a slow day, and I didn't have to be in any hurry. I looked at the two people and saw a young man at one stall and, down a few stalls, was a female. Both were hitting the ball with equal ineffectiveness. I set up in one of the driving stalls, which was as far away from both of the other people as possible, and started limbering up and swinging my seven iron. A short time later, the young man became obviously upset with his performance at hitting the golf balls, and he gathered his things and strolled back to the clubhouse.

I started hitting a few balls with the seven iron and progressed up to my woods. I had been playing golf for a few years and was carrying a twelve handicap. Most of my shots with my woods were carrying out between two hundred to three hundred yards, straight away.

As I was hitting my woods, I became aware the female had stopped hitting balls and was watching me intently. I continued hitting balls and was startled when the female walked up to me.

"How in the world do you hit so well?" she asked. "Do you mind if I watch you for a while?"

"Oh, just comes with years of practice" I said.

"Hi, I'm Jake and, no, I don't mind if you watch. What's your name?"

"Melinda. Glad to meet you. It won't make you nervous or mess you up if I watch?"

"I guess that depends upon how long you watch and if you start criticizing me," I laughed.

"I don't see how I would be able to criticize you," she said in a soft dreamy voice.

"Are you in the Air Force?" she asked.

"Used to be; now I'm a DoD civilian."

"What are you doing on Guam?"

"I'm here on a business trip. I work with computers, and I'm here to see if I can solve the problems the base has been having with some of theirs. I just had some free time today and decided to get in some golf."

"Where're you from?" she asked.

"I live in the Washington, D.C. area. And you? Where're you from?" I asked.

"Well, my home now is anywhere the Air Force sends me. But I'm originally from the Detroit, Michigan area," she replied.

"What do you do that you can be on the golf course in the middle of the day?" I asked.

"I work the night shift in the photo analysis office here on Anderson.

We provide photo interpretation support for the BUFF's."

"BUFF's?" I asked

"You know, the B-52D's. Some people refer to them as BUFF's – Big Ugly Flying #%@*ers."

"Oh," I said, surprised at her forwardness. "I guess I'd never heard that nickname for them. Is that what has been making all that noise around here?"

"Yeah, they're conducting Operation Arc Light, which is the bombing of North Vietnam. Their missions typically last for ten to twelve hours, with in-flight aerial refueling. They are very well loaded down with munitions when they take off. They normally use the entire runway to get airborne; they are so heavy. You should see the black smoke billowing out of those engines as they struggle to get off the ground. Haven't you ever seen one taking off?"

"No, I haven't. But I'm sure that I'll get a chance while I'm here on Anderson," I replied. "So, you are in the Air Force. Are you enlisted or officer?"

"I'm a staff sergeant."

I returned to hitting a few more balls and then began to capitalize on the situation.

"I noticed that you weren't doing all that bad hitting the ball," I said.

"You're just being very nice, and I warn you that flattery will get you everywhere," Melinda said.

"Is that right? Well then, I should guess a golf lesson might get me exactly where I want to be."

"And where might that be?" she cooed.

"Oh, out on a date with you would be a great place to start!"

I hadn't really looked that close at Melinda prior to that moment. Oh, I had noticed the nice figure, the red hair, and the fine butt as she had been swinging those golf clubs, but I hadn't taken the time to look real close. As I now gave her the once over, I saw the beautiful blue eyes, the full pouty lips, the immaculate skin, the dark red hair, the rounded shoulders and the ample breasts hinted at by the narrow cleavage showing where her blouse was unbuttoned at the top. The slim hips highlighted her small waist and the rather long well-formed legs that were neither too small nor too large.

By the time I had gotten down to the trim ankles, Melinda had looked at me with an equally unveiling observation and was looking me right in the eyes when I looked up.

"Well?" she said, "Does it all meet with your approval now that you have visibly looked beyond my outfit with those x-ray eyes?"

"One of the best 9.9's I have seen in a very long time."

"Only a 9.9?" She said. "I take it that is a value rating. If it is, how high does the rating go? And should I feel somewhat slighted?"

"I'm sorry, that is my personal rating system for women. The top is a 10! I don't normally give anyone a perfect 10," I said.

"What would it take to get that 10?"

"We can discuss that in detail after the golf lesson and dinner tonight."

After moving to the practice tee where Melinda had been before we began talking, I had her tee up a ball and get into her normal stance.

"What iron are you using?" I asked.

"I have the five iron," she replied.

"Then you need to be addressing the ball with it slightly back of the center of your stance. For your higher numbered clubs, you should have the ball more towards your right foot. As you move down in the numbered clubs, you move your stance so the ball is more towards your left foot. Now, take a swing at the ball."

I watched her backswing, contact with the ball and her follow through. The ball hooked off to the left and went about seventy-five yards.

"Your problem is in your backswing and ball contact," I said.

I moved in close behind her and put my hands on her arms. As I lightly pressed against her, I felt her push into me.

"We aren't going to get much golf accomplished if you continue to do that, but the pro-shop personnel might enjoy watching the action out here," I whispered into her ear.

I slowly moved her arms into the proper backswing motion and stopped her at the top of the backswing.

"Now," I said, "you start your hips moving to the left shortly before you start your downswing. When the club head gets to the ball, the clubface should be perpendicular to the ball, and your hips should be slightly ahead of your club. Don't look up yet, but keep your eye on the ball as the club makes contact with it.

"After you hit the ball, follow through with your arm swing, and that'll force your head up, and your eyes can then observe the flight of the ball. Finish by completing the follow through, and the club will end up over your left shoulder with your arms bent at the elbows."

Melinda took several swings with the five iron, and her ball went straightaway and about one hundred and twenty yards. She tried several more swings with different clubs and improved with each one.

"Let's get out on the course and see how you do," I said.

We played nine holes and both did well. I hit a forty-one, and Melinda hit a fifty-eight. At the end of the nine holes, she stated that she had some things to do and would have to go. I tried to talk her into another nine holes, but she refused saying that she really needed to go.

"That offer for dinner still on?" she asked.

"You bet!"

"When and where?"

"Well, I'm staying here on Anderson and will need to go get cleaned up. Where'd you like to go?"

"The Hilton has one of the best bars and restaurants on the island, and I don't work tonight," she replied.

"Shall we say around 7:30 pm at the Hilton?"

"You're on. I'll see you then. Want to meet in the bar?"

"The bar it is," I said.

I was extremely proud of myself. Not only had I gotten in a round of golf, managed to relax and get the mission off my mind, but I had also met a very nice young woman in the process.

My lucky day, I hope the night goes even better, I thought to myself.

I glanced at my watch and saw it was 1:20 pm. I walked over to the clubhouse and found a telephone. I called the airport and spoke to the Immigration and Customs Supervisor on duty. Even though I was not expecting Subject yet, I had to continue to go through the efforts to keep them watching for me.

With that done, I finished the second nine holes and was in such a state of bliss that I couldn't seem to do anything wrong. I shot a thirty-nine and was very pleased with my day.

It was a little after 4:00 pm when I finished golf. As I started back towards my room, I heard the sound of what I now expected to be a BUFF taking off. Therefore, as I exited the golf course and headed back towards the main part of Anderson, I stopped near the end of the runway. As I looked out over the runway, I could see one of the mighty B-52D's taxiing down the ramp towards the end of the runway. I decided to sit and watch this one take off.

As it came around the end of the taxiway, it stopped for a few minutes. All of a sudden, with a deafening roar, the eight engines started bellowing black smoke, and the aircraft started rolling. Louder and louder got the roar of the engines as huge billows of black smoke rolled away from it on both sides. It just kept going down the runway. I thought it was never going to lift off. Just as suddenly as it had started rolling, it slowly lifted itself off the runway with a graceful movement not expected from such a giant. Even after it got airborne, it appeared to linger over the ground for what seemed to be a long time. It slowly and gracefully gained altitude, still billowing huge clouds of black smoke all the time. I watched it until it went out of sight, up into the clouds in the sky. *What a magnificent sight,* I thought to myself. That was well worth a few minutes of my day. I wondered about the crew on board and where they might be headed on that long flight. In my mind, I wished them well and *Godspeed.*

A B-52 taking off from Anderson AFB, Guam circa 1972
Courtesy of the U.S. Air Force

CHAPTER 4

It was only 6:00 pm when I finished straightening up my room and getting cleaned up and ready for the evening. I put on a pair of khaki slacks and a red short-sleeved shirt. The shirt was unbuttoned at the top and showed the top of my dark chest hair.

Damn, I am sure good-looking, I whispered to myself with a grin and chuckle as I looked in the mirror. I was ready for the evening. I would drive down to the Hilton and have a nice slow drink while I waited for Melinda.

As I walked into the bar, it took a few seconds for my eyes to adjust from the bright outside to the low light level and intimate setting in the bar. There were only a couple of older people sitting at the bar. They were in a deep discussion and weren't aware that I even walked in. No one else was in the room except for the bartender, whose nametag said Marge. She was a slender woman in her mid-thirties. Although she still looked rather nice in her tight jeans and low-cut red halter top that more than showed enough of her ample bosoms, she had obviously put many miles on that body. I did not want to be known, since I may have to run my operation here at the Hilton, so I didn't call her by her name.

"Good evening, sir, what'll you have?"

"How about a JD and water in a tall glass?"

"Coming right up."

As the woman prepared my drink, I glanced around the rest of the room.

There was a Wurlitzer Jukebox at the edge of a small dance floor in the back corner, some tables and chairs in the center of the room and a few dark leather covered booths along the walls. I had decided on a booth in the corner near the jukebox when the bartender sat the drink on the bar with a napkin.

"That'll be $3.50," she announced.

"Darn, that's a mite bit steep, isn't it?"

"Everything is higher than a giraffe's hind end here on Guam. We don't grow anything except coconuts and jungle, so everything has to be brought in. Have you tried eating out yet?"

"Now that you mention it, I did think I was being robbed. I think I paid $4.50 for a hamburger."

"Yeah, well get used to it. You here to stay?"

"No, just on a business trip."

"Well when you get back to the mainland, I guess you'll get away from these high prices."

"Yes, but we don't have the great weather year round."

"Yeah, we've got to have something going for us."

I paid for the drink and walked over to the jukebox. I put in several quarters and punched in some numbers. Before I could finish and sit down, the blaring refrain of CCR's "Proud Mary" startled me, and everyone in the room. From somewhere behind the bar, Marge quickly turned down the volume to a more reasonable level.

I slid into the booth and sat my drink on the table.

Almost immediately, my mind drifted back to my days at the OSI Basic Investigators Course in Washington, D.C. and the nights at the Neon Moon in Silver Springs, Maryland. After "Proud Mary," a string of other CCR, Elvis, Otis Redding and Janis Joplin tunes played.

I was so deep in thought that I didn't even notice Melinda slide into the booth across from me. As she softly whispered hello, it startled me and returned me to the present. I looked across the table at her and instantly melted into a pile of blubbering mush. She was wearing a low-cut pink blouse that highlighted her blue eyes and shoulder length red hair.

I tried to speak but could only utter an unfamiliar string of unintelligible sounds. Melinda looked at me in disbelief and spoke in a voice that seemed a hundred miles away.

"Did I interrupt your thoughts, or do you always speak so incoherently to ladies in a bar?" she asked.

"Oh my goodness, Melinda, I'm so sorry. I guess I was several years and about eight thousand miles away."

"And where would that have been?"

"The music had me in one of my favorite dance halls at a time I was going through some very intensive training and needed a place to unwind."

"Well, you really must have been enjoying yourself in that dream as I have never heard such dribble coming out of anyone's mouth in all my life."

"Sorry, what would you like to drink?"

"How about a Tequila Sunrise, stiff?"

As she said that, Marge had walked up to the booth and said, "Coming right up."

We finished about half of our first drinks and completed a lot of small talk – our likes and dislikes, what we wanted from life, etc.

The jukebox started on a new song. It was the Righteous Brothers singing "Unchained Melody," one of my all-time favorite tunes.

"Care to dance?" I asked.

"I thought you were never going to ask," she replied.

We went out on the dance floor, and I took her hand and pulled her close. She didn't resist as our bodies became like one, moving slowly around the dance floor in a sensuous rhythmic single motion. Time stopped, and our minds melted together. Melinda slowly moved her head away from my shoulder and stared into the deep recesses of my mind through my eyes.

"I haven't felt this strongly for anyone in a very long time," she said in a soft faraway voice.

I looked down into her angelic face and slowly pressed my lips against her lips in a long lingering kiss.

Marge broke the silence and hollered, "Hey you lovers, the music stopped two minutes ago, you ready for another round?"

The sudden sound brought us both back to reality and, in embarrassment, I said in a sheepish voice, "Sure."

We lingered a while longer listening to music and finishing our second drink.

I asked, "Are you ready to eat dinner?"

"Do we … really need to?" she asked in a slow halting voice.

"Yes, I'm starved and after that dance I feel drained."

We went to the hotel restaurant and looked over the menu and wine list. "Would you like to have fish, red meat or fowl," I asked.

"I think I'm tasting fish tonight."

"Would you like me to order for you?"

"That'd be nice," she said in a smooth soft voice.

When the waiter came, I ordered two Mahi Mahi dinners served on a bed of seasoned rice with steamed vegetables and a small dinner salad with blue cheese on the side. For the wine, I asked the waiter what he would recommend.

"We have an excellent 1969, Chardonnay that should go well with your dinner, sir."

"That was a very good year, at least for me. We'll try it."

After eating rather slowly and enjoying the food and more small talk, I asked, "Do you want me to get a room here tonight?"

She did not bother to answer but simply said, "I'll wait by the elevator."

I paid the bill, walked over to the front desk, and obtained a room.

I then walked to where she was standing.

"You know," I said, "I really think a nice walk out around the pool, and maybe a look at the beach, would be relaxing before we go upstairs."

"I agree I love the smell of the ocean at night."

After a few minutes outside in the cool evening air, we walked back inside and to the elevators. As I pushed the UP button, she placed her hand into mine and looked up at me with a dreamy smile.

When I opened the door to the room, the lights were on low, a radio was playing softly and the bed was pulled down with two small chocolates on the pillows.

"Darn, now that's service," I exclaimed.

"What an absolutely wonderful evening," Melinda said, as she stretched her neck upwards, and slowly sealed my mouth with those beautiful lips.

Somehow, that night, I forgot to make my 11:45 pm call to the airport.

The next morning, as I gently kissed her to wake her up, I whispered into her ear, "Good morning, my number 10!"

CHAPTER 5

Over the next two days, Melinda and I spent a lot of time together. She showed me all of the tourist spots on the island, and we enjoyed the beautiful white Tarague Beach, which is accessed from within Anderson AFB. We even drove the entire thirty miles around the island. The miles of mangroves, tangan-tangan brush and coconut palms were beautiful.

In addition, I even managed to complete all of the necessary work commitments I needed to.

It was during those two days in January 1972, the world was shocked at the news of a World War II Japanese Imperial Army soldier being captured in the jungles of Guam. A couple of Guamanian hunters had found Sergeant Shoichi Yokoi. He had been hiding in a tunnel-like underground cave in a bamboo grove in the Talofofo Jungle for twenty-eight years, since the end of WWII. His story amazed the entire world, and there was much notoriety surrounding him. Of course, everyone on Guam was talking about it everywhere we went. Yokoi had been an apprentice tailor prior to being drafted into the Army in 1941. When he was caught, he was wearing clothing he had made from the fibers of wild plants. He had arrived on Guam in February 1943. After the Americans successfully landed on Guam, Yokoi's unit was close to having to fight to the last man when he and several others fled into the mountains. Eventually Yokoi ended up in the underground cave near the Talofofo River. There had been two others with him for several years but, during the last eight years, he had been alone. He had been told by the Japanese Army to prefer death to being captured alive, but he said, as a Japanese soldier, it was not a disgrace to continue on living. Yokoi was among the last three Japanese holdouts to be found after the end of the Second World War.

(1) Wikipedia

On Friday afternoon, Ed Linz notified me that my operations plan had been approved, and I could go ahead and have Larry start calling Mr. Moore to set up a meeting on Guam. I called Larry and told him to make contact with Moore and let me know as soon as that had been done.

On Saturday morning, Larry left a message for me to call him. When I called, Larry advised he had not been able to talk to Moore yet but had left a message that he needed to talk to Moore soon.

The message on Moore's answering machine had implied he was traveling to the Far East and would be back in a week or so.

"Larry, what do you think about the probability that if Moore was traveling to the Far East, he just might make an unannounced stop on Guam?" I asked.

"The possibility of that happening could be very real. I feel strongly it could very likely happen and think we need to be prepared for it."

"I need to check on arriving flights from the other direction," I said.

I told Larry I needed to call my headquarters and advise them of the situation. When I called Ed to explain the new development, Ed simply said, "Break a leg, oh, I guess that's going to be an arm, isn't it?"

"Thanks for the headquarters humor and for getting the operation approved," I replied.

I called Melinda and cancelled our lunch for the day. I told her I would call her later, as something had come up with work. I then called Larry and asked him to meet me at the Naval Hospital in an hour.

By the time we met at the hospital, I had already talked to HM-1 Guyer, and told him today was the day. Therefore, when Larry arrived, we went directly to the lab where the work was to be conducted. Tad had seen the Nagra recorder previously but had not met Larry until then. Since Larry was somewhat thin, with fairly small arms, Tad felt it wasn't going to be difficult to hide the recorder inside a cast. He placed an elastic bandage material over Larry's arm first so the metal recorder would not chafe his arm.

Next, the recorder was secured in place with another piece of elastic material. Tad then fabricated the plaster of Paris cast over the recorder and Larry's arm. The cast became somewhat larger than it normally might have been, and we were concerned at first. However, HM-1 Guyer had been able to include some additional material around the recorder so that its presence was not noticeable. I had taken pictures of the entire process so I could include them in my report. After the corpsman was through with the process, the cast was allowed to dry for about thirty minutes.

Larry stated he was somewhat uncomfortable, as the plaster of Paris material was getting very warm. I told him it probably was nothing compared to how hot his arm would get in the tropical heat of Guam.

"Thanks for all of your encouragement, Jake," Larry replied.

After thirty minutes, Larry was asked to try to turn on and off the recorder. I had a separate piece of equipment to tell if the recorder was on or not. Everything worked just fine. Larry was assured the battery life of the recorder would allow it to operate for more time than would be needed.

We completed everything, and I told Larry to be sure he had his story straight about how he broke his arm. We then departed the Naval Hospital with Larry being reminded to call me immediately if Mr. Moore made contact.

Saturday afternoon, I met with Capt. Byer and told him of the possible change of timing for the black market operation. I told him that, due to the potential for critical timing in the next two weeks, I felt we should conduct the theft of monies operation the next day, which would be a Sunday, if we were going to be able to do it at all.

"Do you really want to even try to do this little thing?" he asked.

"Sure, it won't take much of my time, and it's already been approved by HQ. Besides, it will buy you some goodwill on the base, and I love catching crooks! Do you think you can set it up with Lt. Bockron on this short of notice?"

"I'm sure he will jump at the chance to catch this guy and improve his overall money intake," Byer answered.

"OK, just let me know as soon as you can. I'm ready for it."

At about 4:30 pm Saturday afternoon, Shaun Byer called and said the monies theft job was on. I was to meet Lt. Bockron in the parking lot outside of the community center at 10:00 pm on Sunday. He would let me into the center and then leave. I was to pick the locks on the six pinball type machines and one jukebox. After I opened the machines, I was to make an exact count of the money by coin denomination, photograph everything and then close them up. When I was all through, I was to let myself out of the community center and then bring the report to Capt. Byer on Monday morning after his command briefing.

Everything worked out perfect with Melinda and me. We were able to spend part of Saturday evening together and all day Sunday. She had to work both nights, so I was free to accomplish what I needed to do.

Sunday night I met Lt. Bockron at the prescribed time.

"Thanks for taking care of this for us," Bockron said as we met in the parking lot. "I know this isn't a big deal for you, but it is something that has been bothering me for quite some time now. It'll be good to just get it over with."

"No problem at all," I replied. "I'm happy to be able to assist you and Capt. Byer."

He let me into the community center and pointed out the machines I needed to work on. At that point, he departed, and I was on my own.

A quick glance at the six pinball machines revealed they all had simple wafer-style locks and would be easy enough to pick. The jukebox could be a different story, as it was a pin-tumbler lock, which might be harder to pick.

I set to work on the pinball machines. As I had expected, the locks picked with relative ease, and I was inside each one of them in only a couple of minutes. A slow, deliberate count of the exact amount of coins in each machine by denomination took a little longer. For each machine, when all of the coins had been counted and stacked on a table, I then photographed the coins, then returned them to the moneybox and closed the machine.

After about one and a half hours, I was through with the pinball machines. I moved over to the jukebox, and luck was with me this night. The pin-tumbler lock almost opened itself. I made the count of coins, photographed them and locked the jukebox back up.

A quick look around to make sure everything was exactly as I found it, and I was out the door and headed towards my VOQ room. The whole process had taken me a little over two hours. On Monday morning, I provided Capt. Byer with the results of my operation.

Byer later told me that with the coin counts and photos I provided, Lt. Bockron was able to confront his assistant on Monday when he turned in the monies for the weekend. His totals for the weekend reflected a shortage of fifty dollars. When Bockron asked the assistant if that was all of the money that had been in the six pinball machines and the jukebox, the assistant stated, yes, it was all he got from the machines. Bockron then showed the assistant the photos and lists I had provided and told him where the photos and list came from and how they were obtained. The assistant at that point admitted to the thefts and was turned over to Capt. Byer. In pursuing the investigation, Byer was able to determine that based upon the value of the missing money from the weekend and the statement from the assistant, a probable total of approximately one hundred dollars per week had been taken by the assistant for the past six months. That amounted to approximately twenty-four hundred dollars total. Not bad for a little extra change!

CHAPTER 6

The next two weeks were both heaven and hell for me. Every day, I made my calls to the airport at 1:30 pm and 11:45 pm. I talked to Larry at least two times a day and called Ed at least twice a week. And we waited for the possible call from Mr. Moore.

At other times during the day and some evenings, I spent as much time as possible with Melinda. The bad part of that was she seemed to be getting serious about our relationship. Not that that was bad, but when this case was completed, I would be back in Washington, D.C., and she would still be on Guam. Our time together always went so fast, and she could not understand why I needed to make so many calls each day. "Just business," I would tell her. "I'm trying to make enough money to be able to spend it all on you." Our time together was spent on the golf course, the beach and in romantic rendezvous.

After two weeks, Moore finally called Larry and advised he had not been able to stop on Guam and would try to get back there on his next trip in that direction.

I called Ed with the news. "Ok, then, shut the operation down and get back here ASAP," said Ed. "We're tired of financing your vacation to the tropics."

If he only knew the truth, I thought.

Larry and I agreed the "broken arm" needed to stay in the cast for at least another week to sell the cover story.

I had arranged with HM-1 Guyer to carefully cut open the cast and remove the Nagra so I could take it back with me.

The cast could then be wrapped with a couple more layers of gauze and plaster of Paris to make it look the same. Larry had not let anyone sign it.

At this point, I decided I needed to tell Capt. Byer about Melinda. I wanted someone on Guam to know about her and what she meant to me. I also wanted someone to keep an eye on her for me and to give her any help she may need. I called Shaun and asked if he had a few minutes for me to brief him on the latest situation with the operation.

"Sure, Jake, do you want to stop by the office?"

"I'll be there in five minutes," I replied.

When I arrived at the OSI Building, Shaun was in his office. "May I come in?" I asked.

"Of course, what's up, Jake?"

I told him of the phone call from Mr. Moore to Larry. "So, nothing is going to happen with this operation for now," I stated. "We're going to brief the IRS when I return to D.C. and see if they want to continue to try to catch Mr. Moore. I've a feeling they'll want to keep going, so I think I'll be returning to Guam again in the near future."

"Sounds to me like you're probably correct, what does HQ think about it?"

"They want to get a full briefing and then to talk to the IRS but, so far, they think it'll still be a go. We'll keep you informed of any changes," I said.

"There is one other thing I need to tell you. Since I have been here this past month, I've met a wonderful young woman who I have become very fond of. Her name is Melinda Scott. She is a staff sergeant and works in the photo analysis office here on Anderson. I must tell you, no one back in D.C. knows about this yet, as I did not want them to have any reason to question anything I was doing here. My involvement with Melinda has in no way affected any part of the operation, I assure you. My request is for you to please keep an eye on her for me while I'm gone."

"Wow, Jake, that sounds pretty serious. I'm happy for you and must tell you I'd seen you with a young woman here on base. At the golf course, in fact. I didn't say anything to you, as I figured it was your business, and I did not want to interfere. Of course, I will watch out for her. Do you want to tell her about me so we could keep in touch?"

"No, she doesn't even know that I'm an OSI agent yet. She only knows the cover story and has been happy with that so far. I didn't want to take any chance in compromising the operation and thought I'd tell her the truth about me at a later date, especially if I might be coming back soon to work the operation again. I feel strongly she'll be alright with the deception and will understand the need for it once I'm able to tell her the full story."

"Have it your way, Jake. I'll watch her for you. That is the least I can do after all you've done here for us."

"Thank you, sir."

As I left, I knew I still had the hard part to do. I would have to tell Melinda my time on Guam, at least for this trip, was through. I knew she was not going to take it very well, and I dreaded having to tell her. We had already agreed to meet at the golf course that afternoon, so I would tell her then.

When I arrived at the golf course, Melinda was on the driving range. She saw me arrive and waved hello. As I walked towards her, without going and renting clubs, I could tell she knew something was wrong.

Darned woman's intuition, I thought as I walked up to her. I tried to put on as big a smile as I could, but it was too late.

"What's wrong? Why the long face, honey," she said.

I just blurted it out, "I've got to go back to D.C."

"When?"

"In three days. I already have my airline reservations."

"Just like that, with no warning, nothing?"

"It's the way my job goes, Melinda. I don't have a lot of control over it."

Just as fast as she had been deflated, she bounced back immediately. "That's OK. We still have three full days, right?"

"Yes, I have all of my equipment packed and ready to go. I was able to tell them I needed three more days to get everything ready for the return trip. I've nothing to do, but spend all my time with you."

I will call in and take three days leave. I don't want anything to interfere with our time."

The next three days were possibly the best three days of my life so far.

We went snorkeling among the coral table reefs off the beautiful beaches. We were lucky enough to see a large green sea turtle and plenty of the royal angelfish.

We also went surfing, played golf, went out to drink and dinners and danced until all hours of the night.

I finally realized I had been bitten and bitten hard. This was the woman I'd been looking for.

In the last afternoon, while we were sitting on the beautiful white sand on Tarague Beach with the tall curved coconut palm trees gently blowing in the soft breeze, Melinda leaned over and gave me a long soft kiss.

"What was that for?"

"Jake, I've got to tell you something, and I'm not sure exactly how you are going to take it. However, it cannot wait any longer. I've fallen head over heels in love with you, like I've never fallen for anyone else in my life."

"Darn, you beat me to it! I have been talking to myself for over an hour, trying to get the words correct and the time right. So, all I can say now is that's how I feel too!"

I leaned over to those lovely lips and drank in her soul with a very soft, lingering kiss.

When I finally broke lip contact, she simply wilted down onto the sand and just lay there with her eyes closed for the longest time with a deep look of contentment like none I had never observed in a woman.

Finally, she opened her eyes and asked in a slow halting voice, "Would you mind … if I put in for a transfer … to the Washington, D.C. area?"

"Mind? Could you? What are the chances of you getting something like that?"

"I can always get a job in the Pentagon again. I was there for three years. I swore that I'd never go back but, if you were there I'd do anything!"

"You have to know that my job takes me away from D.C. sometimes quite often and sometimes for several weeks."

"Yes, I figured that, but I'd still see you a lot more than I ever will again here on Guam."

"Well go ahead and see what the chances are but hold off putting in for the transfer right away. I've a sneaky feeling I'll be back here again soon."

"Really!" Her spirits were flying as high as those BUFF's in only seconds. She jumped up and started running towards the beautiful blue water.

"Last one in has to buy drinks tonight," she hollered as she hit the water.

That evening we spent the time alone in a room at the Hilton. The next morning, we slept in and had a late breakfast in the hotel restaurant. Melinda followed me to the airport and waited as I turned in my rental car.

I checked in for the flight, and then we just sat and talked in the general public area until it was time for me to go to the gate for my departure.

"Please tell me you'll write and call often," she said.

"You know I will. I'll call as soon as I get to D.C."

We kissed and she had big tears as I walked down the gangway and onto the plane. She stood at the window and watched as the plane roared out of sight.

CHAPTER 7

Once I got back to Washington, D.C., I had a lot of debriefing and report writing to do. I had called Melinda as soon as I got home, just as I'd promised. On the first day back in the office, Maj. Point had wanted to know how everything had gone. Point then advised me to go down to OSI Headquarters and brief Col. O'Leary, Maj. Hanson and Ed Linz on the operation. I had advised them all that, according to Larry, the Subject probably would still be meeting the source on Guam, but the time was unknown.

Ed Linz advised he would brief the IRS on the case and see if they wanted to continue to plan on following through with a possible meeting between source and Subject. Of course, they probably would since the potential for recovery of a rather large sum of money from the Subject still appealed to them very much.

After my meeting at OSI Headquarters, Ed asked me to come to his office for a minute.

"Alright, Jake, what happened out there?"

"Well, the operation went very smoothly and I think we would've gotten what we wanted."

"I'm not talking about that, you dummy! You did not keep in touch as you always do. You did not seem to have the operation on your mind. Oh, you did at first. However, after about the fourth day, you changed. What happened? Did you and the source not get along?"

"You mean it was that obvious? Did anyone here say or notice anything?"

"No, just me. I know you too well. I knew something was going on."

"Well it was nothing to do with the operation or the source. I met the most beautiful, wonderful woman in the world!"

"Shut up! You mean it finally happened? Who the heck is she? Was anything compromised about the operation? What does she do?"

"Hold on," I said. "Her name is Melinda Scott. She is a staff sergeant in the U.S. Air Force and stationed at Anderson Air Force Base. She works in the photoreconnaissance section on base, and I am willing to bet she has a Top Secret Clearance. In addition, no, nothing was compromised. She doesn't even know what I do. She still believes the cover story!"

"Well, I'll be darned. So, the great Jake Douglas has finally fallen for someone?"

"How about hurrying up on the contact with IRS. I want to go back to Guam!"

"Hold on there. How do I know you'll pay attention to the operation, and get the job done and not be off moon-eyed with this little lady?"

"Come on Ed, you know me better than that! I may be crazy over Melinda, but I'll always get the job done no matter what!"

"I'll see what I can do. As I told the bosses, I am sure the IRS is going to want this thing followed through. They really want to get some money out of this guy. It'll depend upon the probability the source can talk Subject into a meeting on Guam."

"Work your magic, Ed, and I'll owe you another one!"

"Your account is getting rather long there, ol' buddy. When are you going to figure out how to pay it off?"

"Well, I can see about getting my contact out at Wright-Patterson AFB to come up with some good reason to need a high-priced headquarters weenie for a long operation out there!"

"You know they won't let me go out to the field as long as I'm tied to this darned operations approval desk."

"Maybe, but if I get Melinda transferred to the Washington, D.C. area, I might be interested in taking a desk job."

"I'll get right to work on the IRS!"

"Good man. I better get back out to Maryland and make sure all of my equipment is good-to-go."

"That brings up a good question. Since you surely can't break another of the source's extremities, how do you propose to hide a bug on him this time?"

"I've been thinking about that. I plan to use a transmitter on him this time. I have not figured out exactly how I am going to put it on his body. That will have to be decided when I get to Guam and talk to him. I know we will hide the transmitter somewhere on his body, but I don't know yet where I'll remote the microphone. The source has told me the Subject has never patted him down, so I don't think we have much to worry about in that area."

"Ok, that sounds good. We can work out the details later."

"I'll be in touch soon. Make sure you take enough equipment to get the job done."

"Thanks buddy."

I spent the next two weeks around the office in Maryland. It was very hard to wait on the telephone call from Ed, but I was able to keep myself busy writing the report, deciding what equipment I'd need if I went back to Guam and getting that equipment all checked out and ready to go. Since I would be using a transmitter style bug this time, I would need a reliable method of receiving the transmitted signal and recording any conversation. I decided on a Motorola T-2 transmitter system with a receiver/recorder briefcase. The transmitter came with an elastic waistband battery pack, which contained six 9vdc batteries. The transmitter was approximately ¾" deep x 1 ½" wide x 2" long. It could be low power with a limited battery life since it would only be utilized for a short time. Once the Subject's arrival on Guam was verified, I would meet Larry and install the transmitter prior to any scheduled meeting.

I also managed to call Melinda every day at about 9:00 am her time, which was about 7:00 pm D.C. time. She was usually through working her night shift by then and getting ready to get some sleep. She had checked into a transfer back to the Pentagon and found out there was an opening in her field there, and she was eligible for a transfer in five more months. If she wanted the position, it would be held for her.

Finally, on the third Wednesday after I had returned to D.C., I got a call about midmorning from Ed.

"Pack your stuff, and get on your horse. Larry called IRS and told them Subject called him and stated he would be on Guam in a week and a half! You need to get there and figure out how you are going to pull this thing off.

Since you'll be using a transmitter this time, you'll need to reconnoiter the hotels again to determine how you'll be able to monitor a conversation with a receiver and recorder."

"I knew you'd come through, Ed, so everything is checked out and packed. All I need to do is have Julie Healer make the airline reservations. I will be on my way ASAP."

"Are you still teasing poor Julie about that darned tattoo? How's she doing by the way?"

"Yes, she wouldn't know how to take me if I didn't tease her a little. She's doing fine, but her life is certainly about to change."

"How's that?"

"Well, she's in a family way. She's going to have a baby next April."

"Wonderful. It's about time she started a family. Tell her I said congratulations."

"Oh, and, by the way, Jake, this time spend a little less time with you know who and keep in touch with me a little better."

"You've got it," I said.

CHAPTER 8

On Thursday evening of that week, I was on my way back to Guam. I had called the Immigration & Customs Office at the airport as well as the source and told them the case was back on the front burner. Julie had been able to get me on the 1:00 pm arrival on Friday so Melinda would be there to meet me. I would spend a little bit of time with her on Friday afternoon and then be able to reconnoiter the five major hotels that evening.

"Hi, sweetheart, you look wonderful," Melinda, said as she threw herself into my arms.

"Hello 10!"

We had a wonderful afternoon on Tarague Beach on Anderson, which had become our favorite hide-away.

That evening, after leaving Melinda on base, I completed my reconnoitering of the hotels. I looked at each one, with attention to the bars, restaurants and parking areas with relation to the rooms. Each hotel had their own style of floor layouts. That would present individual problems to me in relation to where I would be able to get good receiver signal coverage of the possible meeting sites. They all could present some real trouble to me if the meeting was conducted in the wrong place. I made notes of the specific trouble areas in each hotel and would brief Larry about where he should attempt to keep the meeting from occurring.

On Saturday, Larry and I met at the Naval Hospital again. We needed to decide how we were going to put the transmitter on him and where we could remote the microphone. There wasn't much of a problem with where the transmitter would be placed. Larry did not feel comfortable, from a security standpoint, with the transmitter being anywhere but in his crotch. Therefore, that answered that question. The waistband battery pack in the elastic band would fit around his waist and under his clothes. As for the microphone, due to the normal tropical weather and plenty of sunshine, Larry always wore sunglasses. He normally carried his sunglasses in a shirt pocket when he was not wearing them. Therefore, I came up with the idea of using a sunglasses case that clipped onto Larry's belt. That way, the microphone could be routed to the case and secreted in the lining of the case. We tried this method, and it worked great.

The last thing to do, to be ready for Mr. Moore, was to get approval for the operations plan from Ed. I sent the message on Saturday evening, and the approval came back on Tuesday morning. However, Ed wanted a significant change to the plan. Since I was using a radio transmitter bug this trip, Ed wanted to have two agents with receivers and recorders to provide better coverage of the meeting. My friend George Carriby had just completed an assignment in Okinawa, and Ed was having George fly to Guam to be the backup agent. George would arrive sometime Wednesday.

The next few days were back to the hurry up and wait routine. There was no choice but to wait for Moore to call Larry and advise when he would be arriving on Guam.

I was making my normal telephone calls to the airport twice a day and keeping in contact with Larry and Ed. I always hated those waiting situations. However, this time it was much easier than normal, as I had someone to be with.

I met George at the airport after the 11:30 pm flight arrived on Wednesday.

"Hey, ol' buddy, how in the world have you been lately?" I asked him.

"Heck, I've been doing real well. I just completed a good theft of base supply materials case over in Okinawa. We were able to bust several airmen and a Department of Defense (DoD) civilian who had a good thing going for themselves in the resale of government supplies."

"Great, what type of equipment did you use, audio or video?"

"I was able to get two Sony AVC 3200 CCTV's mounted in the supply warehouse and one more at the exit dock. We caught the Airmen red-handed moving government equipment out of the warehouse, and they gave up the civilian as the brains behind the whole thing. They'd been getting a lot of GI equipment off base and selling it in the local black market."

"Good job, George. I'm very glad it went so well for you."

We went back to the VOQ where I'd set George up with a room. We had a couple of drinks, and I briefed him on the operation and what his job would be. I also had to tell George about Melinda and ask him to be scarce for the next couple of days if he could.

"No problem," George said. "Does anyone at HQ know of this little wrinkle?"

"Only Ed and he's covering for me."

"Ok, I'll disappear, but I want to meet this little lady that can break down Jake Douglas."

Melinda managed to get a couple more days of leave, so we had plenty of time to be together. When I told her that a friend of mine had come to the island for a few days, she would not have it any other way and wanted to meet him. So, we had breakfast with George the next morning, and I told her George was taking a few days off from a work trip to Japan and spending them on Guam. This time, we just spent a lot of time on the beach and playing golf. We were really enjoying each other's company.

Each day, I went through the formality of calling the airport, Larry and Ed.

On Saturday, a week after I had arrived back on Guam, I spent all day and evening with Melinda. At 11:55 pm, I remembered to call the airport. I was told Mr. Moore had arrived on the 11:30 pm flight!

Panic! I made several calls to Larry but could not get through to him. What was I going to do?

At 1:30 am, Larry called me and advised he had been in the bar at the Cliff Hotel in Agana, when Moore walked in and approached him.

Larry was absolutely shocked and did not know what to do. He told Moore he was just leaving, as he had developed a horrible headache and needed to go home and take care of it.

Moore had cornered him about Larry's stated need for a conversation.

Larry said, yes, he needed to talk, and it was very important. Could it wait until tomorrow? Moore said, yes, and told Larry to meet him in the Cliff Hotel's main dining room at 9:00 am the next morning, on Sunday.

"Aw crap!" I yelled. "That's the worst place and time he could've come up with for my purposes."

"Why is that?" asked Larry.

"9:00 am in the main dining room! Darned, the place will be full of tourists with children, and the noise will be unbearable."

"Well, Jake, there was nothing I could do about it. I was barely able to talk; I was so off guard. I should've expected something like this, as he is famous for just showing up."

"Sounds to me like he's no dummy and is pretty savvy to the possibilities of a surveillance. Oh well, we will just have to do the best we can. When do you want to get the transmitter?"

"I think we better do it tonight, just in case there's any problem with getting together in the morning. He may still call and change the meeting time and/or place. I'll come out to Anderson now, and we can go over everything."

"Ok, I'll see you in a few minutes," I said.

Meanwhile, I called George and woke him up. I told him of the situation and asked him to come over to my room right away.

When Larry arrived, I introduced him to George and explained the need for a second receiver/recorder system.

"We just want to take the necessary precautions to ensure, after all of our preparations, we at least get the recording of the meeting," I said. "I'll be in the dining room with a briefcase. I'll have the T-2 receiver/recorder system in the briefcase and will be within thirty to forty feet from any point in the dining room."

"George will be in a car, located outside of the dining room and about eighty feet from the potential meeting. He will have a more powerful receiver and a Uher 4000 reel-to-reel recorder. He will automatically start recording five minutes before 9:00 am. I'm sure we'll get the meeting recorded, but I'm not at all sure if we'll get any decent audio due to the probable noise level in a dining room of that size on a Sunday morning."

"Ok, everything is as ready as we can possibly get it. Are you sure you can put the transmitter on by yourself and get it turned on?" I asked Larry.

"No problem. But, if I don't go and get some sleep, I'll be a zombie in the morning."

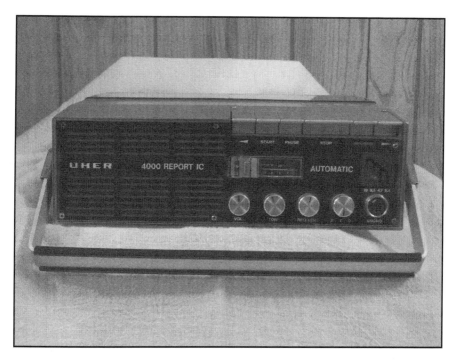

Uher 4000 Audio Recorder – Type used for long-term surveillance recordings circa 1970's Photo by Author.

CHAPTER 9

Sunday morning dawned as a beautiful tropical day. George and I had an early breakfast together, although I only had coffee and a roll, as I would need to eat breakfast in the Cliff Hotel Dining Room to maintain my cover as a guest. We drove to the hotel at about 8:30 am so we would have plenty of time to get into position and be ready for the meeting.

George parked his car in the rear parking lot directly outside and below the dining room, but completely out of sight, and just waited.

I walked around the hotel lobby for a few minutes, and then went into the dining room to be seated. I ordered breakfast and discreetly turned on my receiver/recorder.

At 8:50 am, Larry arrived and managed to have the hostess seat him three tables behind and to my right. I saw Larry enter the room but paid no attention to him in case Moore may have had someone in the dining room watching Larry. As Larry entered the room and was seated, I observed the room occupants to see if anyone was paying any particular attention to Larry. After a few seconds, I managed to glance around the room again to locate Larry.

At 9:05 am, Moore entered the dining room, motioned to the hostess that he was joining someone and walked over to Larry's table.

So, this is the guy that has bilked the military out of millions of dollars, I thought. *He doesn't look rich and certainly doesn't have an air about him.*

The entire meeting and breakfast lasted about one hour. I was able to eat slowly, and read the morning paper, more thoroughly than I had ever read one. I was certainly aware of the general room noise in the dining room but did not remember how much a high quality audio recorder actually heard.

Once the meeting was over, Moore and Larry shook hands and departed the dining room. Larry had been instructed to go to his home and stay there for at least three hours before making contact with me.

I waited about fifteen minutes after the meeting was over before leaving the dining room.

I went back out into the lobby and into the gift shop, where I made sure I was not followed. After another five minutes, I took the elevator up to the third floor, got out, walked down the entire length of the hall and then walked down the rear stairwell and out to my car.

I then drove around town for a few minutes and slowly made my way back to Anderson. By the time I got to my room, George was already there and listening to his audiotape.

"Well, what do we have?" I asked him.

"One heck of a lot of noise and a lot of talking, but I think the boys back at HQ will be able to clean up the tape with that new audio/video enhancement console they got recently."

"Great! I could not hear much except noise myself but knew the microphone in that eyeglasses case should be able to hear what we needed. Let's hear what's on my tape."

I was certainly correct in my expectations. The noise level was high in the dining room. We could hear some of the conversations but just could not make out enough of the words to tell if we had gotten the evidence we needed.

"Again, maybe the guys at HQ will be able to clear up the noise level," said George.

"Let's hope so. Otherwise, we just will not have enough to put this guy away. Let's get these two tapes marked as evidence and complete our surveillance logs."

The next day, we met with Larry at the Naval Hospital and retrieved the transmitter.

"Well guys," stated Larry, "we just basically scored a homerun. I was able to get Moore to admit he had pocketed over eleven million dollars during the black market operation. I guess I caught him in a great mood, and he was so sure of himself in that dining room environment. He just opened up and spilled his guts about the whole thing. I led him along, playing very dumb, asking him various roundabout questions on the way the operation had been run, who he typically sold the goods to, how he moved the goods, how he was able to divert things without suspicion and how much money did he make overall. I was truly surprised he'd even talk about the whole thing."

"We'll see what our guys at Headquarters can do with the audio tapes," I said. "There was a lot of background noise, but we think they can remove enough of it so we can have evidence good enough to hold up in court."

"I hope so guys, because I stand to make a lot of money, at ten percent, if we can convict this guy."

"One thing you should do as soon as you get back home is sit down with pen and paper and write down everything you can remember about the entire conversation with Mr. Moore. That way, you'll have something to refresh your memory with later, if and when you have to testify against this guy."

"Good idea, Jake. I'll go home and do it right now."

"Well, Larry, it has been a pleasure working with you. I appreciate all of your assistance and support and your willingness to do what it took to make this thing happen. With any luck at all, we should be able to make it all worthwhile for you. Take care and best of luck to you."

"Thanks, guys, especially you, Jake. I have really enjoyed working with you, and I've certainly grown to respect all you go through to complete a job. I plan to write a letter to your headquarters expressing my sincere appreciation for your work and professionalism."

"Thanks again. I'll probably see you in court."

All that remained now was to pack everything up and get ready for the return trip to D.C. George was going to stay and travel back with me. Since I would want as much time with Melinda as possible before leaving Guam, George had already told me to go to her, and he'd do all of the packing. It was Monday, and we were able to get a flight out on Wednesday.

Once again, Melinda and I had to say goodbye. It would be a little better this time, as Melinda had put in for the transfer to the Pentagon and would be joining me in the fall. We enjoyed time together and actually spent a fair amount of time with George, as Melinda did not want him to be alone any more than necessary.

On Wednesday, Melinda saw us off at the airport.

As I kissed her goodbye and turned to go, Melinda said, "I love you."

I blew her a kiss and said "too."

CHAPTER 10

Again, once back in D.C. I had a lot of debriefing to complete. Based upon what I told Maj. Point, he was extremely pleased I had done so well. He complemented me on a job well done and stated that I had done him proud.

"Now, go downtown and tell the head shed people your story!" he said.

"I do have one thing that I must tell you now about my time on Guam, sir."

"Yes, what would that be?" he asked.

"Well, sir, while I was on Guam, I met a wonderful young lady, and we have become pretty serious about each other. I do want to assure you nothing about meeting this woman interfered with my operation, and she never knew anything about me except my cover story."

"What does she do, how'd you meet and what's her name?" Point asked.

"She works in the photoreconnaissance section on Anderson AFB. We met one day at the golf course after I had completed all preparation for the anticipated meeting between Subject and source and was waiting for the approval for the job from Ed. Her name is Melinda Scott, and she's a staff sergeant in the Air Force."

"And you can assure me she didn't compromise our operation in any way, Jake?"

"Yes, sir."

"OK, I'm happy you finally found someone to possibly share your life with. Now get downtown and impress those people."

Once I had completed the debriefing of Headquarters technical staff, along with the staff from the Criminal Directorate, everyone was very happy with the outcome of the operation. Headquarters technical lab staff spent quite a bit of time trying to clean up the audiotapes and was able to eliminate enough of the background noises to allow sufficient evidence for possible prosecution of Mr. Moore. They did have several problems trying to get some of the noises out since the frequencies were broad enough that if they completely removed those noises, there would appear to be "gaps" in the tapes. The criminal personnel felt the tapes were good enough to push for a trial and prosecution. That is exactly what they did. Much later, in federal court, Moore was convicted, along with numerous other personnel, of the large-scale black marketing operation he had conducted. He was ordered to pay several million dollars of back taxes to the IRS for income he had never claimed. To protect Larry Owens, he was included in the court case and was given a minimal sentence, since he was considered to have had a minor part in the overall operation. In actuality, he was not prosecuted, based upon his cooperation with the investigation and, in the end, received ten percent of the money that Moore was required to pay the IRS!

A lone B-52D, struggling to maintain altitude, broke through the clouds and sighted the Island of Guam on the horizon. The lone aircraft had been flying for several more hours than normal on its return leg from its bombing run over North Vietnam. This had not been a normal day and certainly not a lucky one!

The pilot, Lt. Col. Tom Purdy, was doing everything he could to get the big bird back to its home base and save those remaining alive on the aircraft. His co-pilot, Major Rick Hardy, was in the right seat but had been injured and had been passing between consciousness, hysteria and blacking out for the past four hours. Purdy had not heard from his tail gunner since just after the bomb run. The bombardier, Major James Sanger was injured, but had refused treatment. Electronic Warfare Officer, Capt. Joe Smith is ok. Navigator, Major Hugh Coffey was also ok and had worked hard to get them this far.

The B-52 had been hit by one SAM Missile and, after losing altitude, had been damaged by Anti-aircraft fire. Two engines had been killed due to fire, and two others were damaged. Purdy had somehow managed to hold the aircraft in the air and keep it somewhat on course for the return to Guam, but it had been a fight. He had released the other B-52's in his formation to go ahead in their return flight to Guam, as he knew he would just slow them down.

As he neared Anderson AFB, he had begun dumping fuel to lighten the load and to make the aircraft as safe as possible, in case it crashed during landing.

"Anderson Tower, this is Bullet two niner two five," Purdy announced on the correct inbound radio frequency.

"Bullet two niner two five, this is Anderson Tower," came back the reply.

"Anderson Tower, Bullet two niner two five, I'm declaring an emergency and requesting a direct approach on Runway 15. I have already been dumping fuel in expectation of a possible landing problem. Do you copy?"

"Bullet two niner two five, Anderson Tower, I copy. We have been expecting you, and all emergency equipment is already in place. You are cleared for a direct approach on Runway 15. How bad are you hit, and what's your crew status?"

"Anderson Tower, Bullet two niner two five. I have rudder damage, right wing damage, two engines killed on the right wing and two engines on the left wing barely working. I haven't heard from the rear gunner since we got hit, and my co-pilot and bombardier are injured, everyone else seems to be ok, copy?"

"Bullet two niner two five, Anderson Tower, copy. What's the status on your landing gear?"

"Anderson Tower, Bullet two niner two five, I really can't tell you the answer to that. I have attempted to lower my landing gear and the indicators say the gear is down and in place. However, I do not remember hearing the gear lock in place. I'm now about twenty miles out from the end of the runway."

"Bullet two niner two five, Anderson Tower, you're on the glide path, but you're a little bit low. Please try to bring your aircraft up at least one hundred feet."

"Anderson Tower, Bullet two niner two five, roger that. I'll try, but she has been fighting me all the way home."

"Bullet two niner two five, Anderson Tower, I've called for the runway to be foamed. Can you try again to lower the gear and lock it, copy?"

"Anderson Tower, Bullet two niner two five, copy and roger that. I am trying the controls again, but I do not hear the gear locking in place. I am raising the gear. It looks like we will be coming in hot and without landing gear. Please hurry with that foaming. ... And pray for us."

"Bullet two niner two five, Anderson Tower, roger that, sir. It looks like you were able to get her up some, so take all the runway you need. We will have the emergency equipment on hand and waiting for you. Godspeed."

"Bullet two niner two five, Anderson Tower, you are slipping to the right of the glide path, please try to correct!"

"Hold on to something guys, we are going in hot with no landing gear. May God be with us."

The mighty aircraft touched down slightly to the left of center of the runway, partially on the grass and partially on the foam and started skidding and angling to the left side of the runway. As it moved further towards the far end of the runway, the left wing suddenly dipped and dug into the turf. The plane shuddered, groaned and started to shift its slide, completely away from the runway, across the taxiway, and towards the parking apron. The pilot took a second to look out the front of the plane to see the direction it was now turning. In the distance, he could see a group of buildings that were clustered too close to the parking apron, and now directly in front of the aircraft. There was nothing he could do but ride the big bird until it stopped. That was the last thing he saw.

CHAPTER 11

After returning to D.C., I had been able to talk to Melinda almost daily. About a month after I got back to D.C., I was called into Maj. Point's office one morning.

"Sit down, Jake; I have some bad news for you."

"What is it, sir?'

"I received a telephone call from Capt. Byer this morning."

"Nothing wrong with him I hope, sir."

"No, but there was an accident on Anderson AFB, last night," he said. "One of the B-52s, returning to Anderson from a bombing mission over North Vietnam, with some heavy damage caused by a SAM missile and some anti-aircraft fire crashed upon landing. It over shot its touchdown point and, without landing gear, it then skidded off the runway. Before it came to a complete stop, it wiped out several of the temporary buildings near the runway. Jake, it hit one of the photo recon buildings. I'm truly sorry to tell you that your girlfriend, Melinda, was working in that building that night and, Jake, she didn't make it."

"Wait a minute Maj. Point. What are you saying?

"Jake, Melinda is dead."

"Oh no, it can't be true. I just spoke to her yesterday evening. She wasn't even supposed to work last night."

"It was one of those unfortunate situations. One of her coworkers was not feeling well, so Melinda volunteered to work in that person's place."

"I'm very sorry, Jake. If you want to take some time off, I certainly understand. Where was she from?"

"Her parents live north of Detroit, in Mt. Clemens," I heard myself reply, but the voice seemed very far away.

"Would you consider possibly going there for the funeral?" Point asked,

"I'll have to take some time to think about that, sir. I believe I will take the next couple of days off."

"Sure, Jake. Is there anything any of us can do for you?"

"No, sir, I'll be fine. I just need some time to think. I'll be at my apartment if you need me."

The next morning, I got a call from Ed Linz.

"Jake, I just heard man. I am truly so very sorry. Anything I can do?"

"Thanks, Ed. No there is nothing anyone can do right now. I have talked to Capt. Byer on Guam, and they will be sending Melinda to her parents' location in a few days. I have decided I owe it to her to go to Mt. Clemens for the funeral and to meet her folks. I've plenty of leave time, and I really need to get away for a while."

"Oh, there's one thing that I hope you can do for me, Ed."

"What's that, Jake?"

"I want a change of scenery and job. I need to transfer to some place where I can throw myself into work and try to forget what has happened. Can you possibly put in a good word for me to transfer some place?"

"I'll certainly see what I can do, Jake. I'll let you know as soon as I find out anything."

Within an hour, I got a call from George Carriby.

"Jake, I just heard. I am so sorry to hear about your loss of Melinda. Even though I only knew her for just a few days, I knew she was the one for you. I can only imagine what you are going through. If there is anything I can do please call on me."

"Thanks, George. I just need some time for now."

"OK. Y'all take care of yourself."

The next couple of days were a blur. I just mainly sat in my apartment, in the dark and, through the tears, remembered the soft voice and touch of Melinda.

I finally made contact with Jim and Maureen Scott. It was difficult, but I knew I had to do it. The phone rang three times before a subdued woman's voice answered, "Hello, this is Maureen who's calling please?"

"Mrs. Scott, its Jake Douglas. I met your daughter Melinda on Guam recently. I hope she mentioned me to you."

Immediately, there was a muffled quiet on the other end of the phone line. Then, I realized it was not quietness at all. It was Mrs. Scott crying and gasping for breath.

"Mrs. Scott, is this a bad time, should I call back later?"

Finally, I heard her say through the sobbing, "No, Jake, I'm sorry. Let me catch my composure for a few seconds."

After a minute or so, I heard her say, "Jake, I'm so very glad you called. Yes, of course, Melinda mentioned you! It was about all we talked about for the past couple of months. I don't think I had ever heard my daughter quite so happy."

"Thank you, Mrs. Scott."

"Maureen, please call me Maureen," she stated.

"Yes ma'am, ah, Maureen. I hate to ask, but have you been told when Melinda will be home. I'd like to come to Mt. Clemens for the service."

"Oh, that would be wonderful, Jake. Jim and I had so hoped to be able to meet you."

After more sobbing, she was finally able to tell me the service would be held in six days.

"Well, I'll be there. Should I fly into Detroit?"

"Yes, that would be the best way. Let us know when you are going to arrive, and Jim and I'll meet you."

"Please, you don't have to do that. I can …" I didn't get to finish.

"We wouldn't have it any other way! We want to spend some time with you and get to know you. We have a guest bedroom and would love for you to stay with us."

"I certainly don't want to be any bother to you especially at a time like this."

"Don't even worry yourself about that. Besides, right now, you are the closest thing to Melinda we have left."

With that, she went back into a fit of uncontrollable sobbing.

"Ok, Maureen, I'll make the arrangements and let you know when I will be there." I was not sure she had heard me but did not want to bother her any more. I would call back later to confirm my arrival.

Five days later, I flew into the Detroit Airport and was met by Jim and Maureen Scott. It was a sobering time. I stayed at their house and was made to feel as family. I had never been in a situation like that and actually enjoyed the attention and welcome. We became closer than I ever thought I could to total strangers. In truth, the strangers feeling only lasted for the first few minutes after we met at the airport.

The next day, the service was held for Melinda. It was conducted with full military honors. I wore my Class A Air Force Uniform and was one of the Pallbearers. It was the most difficult time I'd ever had in my life. I am not ashamed to admit, the tears flowed freely. I stayed with Jim and Maureen for two more days after the service and then had to leave. However, I now have more family in my life and will always keep in touch with them.

Back in Washington, D.C., things in my life just were not the same anymore. Work did not seem to have the same meaning, and I knew I was not as interested in my job as I had been. Col. Point told me he understood and would be as lenient on me as possible.

After I had been back for a week, I got a call from Ed Linz one morning.

"Jake, how about going to Okinawa?"

"Ed, I'm really not in the mood for another job right now."

"No, I mean how about transferring to Okinawa. It's not a bad place to live, and they cover Taiwan and the Philippines so the work can be good. Believe me it's one of the best kept secrets in OSI."

"Oh, I'd almost forgotten I'd asked you to look for a place for me to go. Okinawa, huh? How soon would I get to go?"

"We just had someone leave there early for a humanitarian reassignment, so there is an opening now. You can go as soon as you want to."

"It sounds good to me," I said. "The way I'm feeling right now, I could sure use that sort of change. I'll take it."

"Great, I'll put the move in motion for you. I'll call Maj. Point and speak to him about this. I know he will understand. You should get orders in about a week. You can go ahead and start getting things in order for a move. I think you'll really like it over there, buddy."

My life had changed so much in the past few short weeks. Now, it was going to change even more! I was ready.

OPERATION II: THE DRUG RUNNERS

Location: Kadena Air Base, Okinawa
Allegation: Illegal Drugs Being Transported by Military Aircraft
And Sold by USAF Members

CHAPTER 1

I was aware people were watching JP Mayhews and me with curious looks. Alternatively, was it just that I felt self-conscious about being in this situation? After all, it probably was not every day two people were observed walking around an air terminal, looking up at the large bundle of cables, taking notes and talking about the condition and layout of cables. Even though it was not out of the ordinary for telephone maintenance personnel to be doing their job, I was uneasy as I was working my first undercover operation since I joined OSI. We had to get out of our normal civilian coat and tie and don an Air Force uniform again for the first time in over two years. I was dressed in Air Force fatigues as an airman first class (A1C) and JP was dressed as a technical sergeant (TSgt). We were posing as U.S. Air Force telephone maintenance personnel.

I had met JP when I was transferred from OSI District 4 in Suitland, Maryland to OSI District 41, on Kadena AFB, Okinawa, in July 1972. He had been my sponsor and had done a great job of getting me settled into the new job and location. He had several places for me to look at for possible rental homes when I arrived.

Kadena Air Base Hwy # 1 Entry Gate – Circa 1970 Courtesy of U.S. Air Force

Jack D. Dyer

Kadena Air Base Air Terminal - circa 1975 Courtesy of U.S. Air Force

JP was from the Seattle, Washington area and was married to Mandy. He had a dry sense of humor, and he was often misunderstood as being grumpy. He was very considerate and took great care to train me in all of the ins and outs of the extensive travel we had to do from our base in Okinawa – except for our first TDY to Taiwan! He still swears to this day that I almost got us thrown into jail in Taipei. What he forgot to tell me, before we flew over to Taiwan, was that any "indecent" or "potentially lewd" materials such as a *Playboy* were strictly forbidden to be taken into Taiwan. Therefore, being a young red-blooded American GI, I usually bought and "read" each copy of *Playboy*. Therefore, I thought nothing of taking my latest copy of the magazine in my briefcase with me to Taiwan. Now, when you arrived in Taipei, you went through a very strict inspection of your personal carry-on luggage. That inspection was conducted by the Taiwan military. So, when they opened my briefcase and found the *Playboy*, let me tell you, I thought that all hell had broken loose! There was much chatter, hollering and, I might add, "reading" of the magazine – or I should say the centerfold picture. Of course, the magazine was confiscated and, after much ado, JP and I were allowed to get through the customs inspection.

The next thing that happened on that trip was we were scheduled to go down island to Kaohsiung for some work.

"Great, I said, I will get to see more of the island on my first visit. How will we be traveling?"

"We won't know until after we are able to check in with the air terminal in Taipei to see if there are any U.S. military flights available," JP said.

Later, after our harrowing experience at the airport, we were in for another rewarding experience. There were not any U.S. military flights scheduled within the timeframe that we needed to travel. The Airman in the Operations Office stated that we were in luck though, as there was a Taiwanese Air Force flight scheduled for the next morning, and there was plenty of room on that flight.

"Great," JP said, "what type of plane is it?"

"It is a C-119," the Airman said.

"Wait a minute," I said. "Isn't that one of the old U.S. military's planes that they called the 'Flying Boxcar'?"

"That would be it," the Airman said.

"There isn't any way that I am going to fly in one of those ancient things," both JP and I said at almost the same time.

"They are so old, they must be held together with bailing wire and bubble gum," JP stated.

"So, what other way is there for us to get down to Kaohsiung?" I asked.

"Well, if you don't want to fly Taiwan Air, I guess the only other way to get down island is by train," the airman said.

"Well, that will really give you a great chance to see a lot of Taiwan," JP stated.

"How far is it down island to Kaohsiung?" I asked.

The Airman stated rather bluntly, "About one hundred sixty miles, and it will take you about five to six hours, as the train stops at places that aren't even on the map!"

"Well, it still sounds better that flying in that ancient aircraft that probably needs to have the wings flapping to stay in the air," I said.

Let me tell you, you have not lived in life until you have ridden on any type of oriental train. It is certainly a ride that I will never forget. Not only are the cars very old, but they have small crowded bench type seats with very limited room for anything such as baggage. Moreover, of course, when we traveled as OSI technical agents, we always had numerous, large and heavy metal cases that we had to take with us. So, feature a picture of two guys trying to get all of that luggage onto the train car, within the limited timeframe that the engineer and/or conductor allowed the train to stop. Then, at the same time, fighting all of the other people struggling to get onto the train car with whatever they had such as large cases, bamboo cages with chickens and a whole host of other imaginable objects! Then, we had to jamb all of the cases into a limited space in the rear of the car and, of course, there was only room for one of us to sit where they could watch the cases. So, JP sat in the back with the cases, and I went forward to another empty seat. If you ever have to ride in such a train, I hope that you do not have problems with motion sickness, as those old trains rock back and forth, as they travel down the tracks at what felt like a break-neck speed. The other problem you will immediately have upon getting onto an oriental train is let alone all of the chickens and other possible animals – the people smell, to put it bluntly!

The other experience that I still recall to this day is the person who came around while the train was traveling to hand out steaming hot towels and the other person who came around with the very large metal teapot, small cups and tea bags. The water in the teapot was extremely hot, and very likely would have scalded anyone if the man had missed the cup. However, to my amazement, he never missed a drop! It was truly poetry in motion, as he would move from one person to another, handing out the cups, teabags and then pouring the hot water.

Needless to say, the train ride was one of the most memorable experiences of my life – and we made it to Kaohsiung and back.

One of the first things JP had asked me after I arrived on Kadena was, "Hey, tomorrow for lunch do you want to go over to the golf course restaurant and watch the Habu come in?"

"Come on, I wasn't born yesterday." I replied. "Is that like going snipe hunting? I've been there before!"

"What the heck are you talking about?" he said in an indignant voice. "Don't you know what the Habu is?"

"Apparently not, but I'm sure that you're going to enlighten me."

"The Habu is the Okinawan name for the SR-71 Blackbird. The Habu is a very deadly snake here on the island. Someone decided due to its nature, Habu would be a very appropriate name for the SR-71."

"Oh, I'm sorry. I thought for sure you were just trying to screw with the new guy. So, why do we go to the golf course restaurant to see it?"

"Mainly due to the fact that the restaurant sits up on a small hill and overlooks the west end of the runway. Also, because almost every day, the Habu comes back from its morning flight at just about noon. At about a quarter of twelve, you will see any departing airplanes lining up on the taxiways. They have to wait for the Habu to land before they can even get close to the active runway.

"At about ten minutes till noon, you'll see a pick-up truck drive down the runway, making a foreign object damage "FOD" check looking for anything lying on the runway. Then, at almost exactly noon, you will see the Habu come in, usually from the west. It will touch down and taxi very quickly to the far end of the runway and right into its hangar.

Sometimes, I assume, if it has very valuable data you'll see it fly over the runway at about a couple of hundred feet, drop a box attached to a parachute, then stand itself up into a big loop while the box and parachute are being retrieved and then it'll land."

"Sure, I'd love to see the SR-71, ah Habu, return."
"OK then, we'll go to the golf course for lunch tomorrow."
From that day on, going to the golf course to see the Habu became a favorite pastime of mine. Moreover, on many occasions, I saw the small parachute come out of the Habu, before it landed. Good work guys!

Kadena Air Base Golf Course/Restaurant - circa 1975   Courtesy U.S. Air Force

SR-71 Blackbird (Habu) Courtesy U.S. Air Force

Being on Okinawa in Mid-1972 was quite an experience. After twenty-five years of U.S. occupation and rule, the island had reverted to Japanese rule on June 15, 1972. From what I heard, the six to twelve months before reversion had been extremely chaotic on the island. The Okinawans had been building everything they could during that time, as they knew the Japanese would apply a very high tax on any new building permits after reversion. In addition, the local unions had been protesting everywhere on the island during those six to twelve months, especially near all of the U.S. military bases. Some of the protests had gotten out of hand at times, with serious interruptions of local U.S. off-base schools and U.S. military base entrances. After reversion, the Okinawans had a difficult time with the use of the Japanese Yen, as all they had known for the past twenty-five years was the U.S. dollar.

I had been in OSI for a little over three years now. After the big black-market job I completed on Guam and the terrible loss of Melinda Scott, I'd requested my friend Ed Linz help me get a transfer anywhere away from the Washington, D.C. area. Ed had told me one of the best-kept secrets in OSI was the assignment to Okinawa. It was not bad living and with the geographical area covered by that district, they typically received some good cases to work on. Therefore, here I was. I had been here for about two months, and we were already working on a big case.

JP and I were requested to attend a briefing in the OSI District 41 Criminal Division two weeks ago. Capt. Ryan Barker and the handling agent for this case, Mike Miley, had advised us they had received information from the OSI District 42 Office at Clark Air Base, in the Philippines, about a potential case involving the possible use of USAF Aircraft to transport illegal drugs to Okinawa.

They briefed us on what was known about the operation, which included the suspicion drugs were somehow being routed through the Lost Baggage Office on Okinawa. They asked if we could assist them with technical support in the form of a wiretap.

We stated we should be able to do that and all we needed was the approval of an operations plan by OSI Headquarters and the special equipment we would need to do the job.

That was two weeks ago, and here we were already deep into the job. It had only taken a few days for my friend Ed Linz to get the approval for the wiretap, especially since it would be on base and involve only military personnel.

He had sent us the wiretap equipment we would need, in advance of the approval, so we could get started quickly once approval had been obtained.

As JP and I moved down the air terminal hallway today, checking cables, I saw a rather nice looking woman, with red hair, dressed in civilian clothes, come out of an office down the hall from where we were standing. She had been moving with determination, as if she was certainly going somewhere in particular and in a hurry. She stopped short, and looked at us.

"May I ask what you're looking for?" she said in a voice of authority.

"May I ask why you ask?" It was JP who jumped into the situation before I could even get any words out of my mouth.

"I'm Michele Myer, and I'm the building supervisor. I usually know what's going on in my building," the woman said, again in a voice of authority, but this time in an even sterner voice.

"Yes Ma'am, we're from the telephone maintenance office. We got a call from the Lost Baggage Office that their phone wasn't working," I said, with all of the charm I could muster.

"Oh, that's right," she said. "I remember those idiots mentioning something to me about their phone. I never know with those two people. That's why they are working in that office. We do not have anywhere else they can be trusted not to mess things up. They probably knocked the thing off the desk and broke it."

Man, if she only knew how correct she was, as that is exactly what we will tell the guys the problem is, I thought.

"That's what we're here to find out," I said. "We just wanted to look to be sure there aren't any visible cable problems."

"OK, thanks for handling this problem for me," she said.

CHAPTER 2

JP and I continued down the hall towards the Lost Baggage Office. All the time, looking up at the bunch of cables tied up in the top corner of the hall and commenting about things and taking notes.

As we came to various cable junction boxes, we would stop, open them up and attach our "butinski" (Telephone Lineman's Portable Handset) to several terminals to appear to be checking out certain telephone wires. Sometimes we would make comments about the circuit being ok at that point.

At other times, we would comment about how sloppy someone had been putting in the wiring. Our actions and comments were only meant to throw off anyone who might have been listening to the two telephone men in the hall.

As we continued down the hall, getting closer to the target area, we would continue to make worthless comments about the circuits.

"I bet the problem is going to be in the telephone itself," said J P.

"You're probably correct," I replied.

We were playing this thing right up to the hilt, as our operations plan had called for.

If anyone had been watching us, other than a real telephone maintenance person, it would have appeared as if we knew exactly what we were doing.

As we got to the door of the Lost Baggage Office, JP said, "Well, everything checks out good to here."

"Yeah, I'll bet the lady was right all along," I said.

"Hey, it's ten o'clock let's go get some coffee before we finish finding this problem," said J P.

"OK, I could sure use a cup," I replied. "Besides, it'll give us a chance to see what kind of women hang out in this place,"

"Good idea, you know there are always nice looking women in air terminals," JP said as his face lit up with a big grin.

Later after a couple of cups of coffee, and viewing several women in the terminal, we returned to the Lost Baggage Office.

During our break, we had discussed what had occurred to bring us to where we were today. A trusted source, on Clark Air Base, had told his OSI handling agent, Jerry Mathis, he believed drugs were being smuggled into Okinawa from somewhere in the Far East. Mathis had contacted his counterpart, Mike Miley, in the Criminal Investigations Division, in the OSI Office on Kadena. The source, Leroy Smith, worked in an office in the 13th Air Force Headquarters, on base at Clark. Smith had been recruited, by one of the personnel in the Lost Baggage Office at the Kadena AB Air Terminal, to provide the names of personnel "Killed in Action" (KIA) in Viet Nam. Smith was considered by Mathis to be a motivated source, as Smith did not feel he was being paid enough for the information he was providing. Mathis had tasked Smith to determine as much as he could about the operation. Two weeks later the source had set up a meeting with Mathis.

"The drugs are going into Okinawa on military C-130 aircraft," stated Smith. "The flights were originating in Thailand."

"As best as I can tell by talking to SSgt White, who works in the Lost Baggage Office at Kadena, someone at the originating location would put the drugs into regular suitcases, tagged with the name of a known KIA. Then they make sure the baggage gets put onto a C-130 going straight to Kadena. When the baggage isn't claimed at Kadena, it gets taken to the Lost Baggage Office, where it simply disappears after a short time."

Smith was able to determine the smuggling operation had been going on successfully for quite some time. He opined that since the smugglers had been so successful, they had in fact gotten quite complacent about the operation.

"Do you know what kinds of drugs are being smuggled?" asked Mathis.

"I don't know for sure," Smith replied, "but White has offered me some marijuana as payment and once when I was talking to White on the telephone I did overhear part of a conversation between him and another guy and they mentioned cocaine."

"Do you know how many people are involved in the operation?" asked Mathis.

"I get the feeling the whole operation is conducted by only a couple of people on both ends," replied Smith. "The people on the sending end must work in the outgoing baggage department, and have the capability of making sure the bogus baggage actually gets onto the correct aircraft. The two people, who run the Lost Baggage Office at Kadena, apparently do not have close supervision and are able to ensure the bogus luggage arrives in their office. Therefore, the chance of the operation being discovered is small, and the people are making lots of money."

After that meeting, Mathis had relayed the information to Miley. Then after Mike Miley had briefed JP and me on the operation, I had been tasked with setting up an operations plan and getting the required OSI Headquarters authorization for the plan. Since I knew where the drugs were arriving, that simplified the plan significantly.

All I had to do was find out when the shipments were made and the general operation of the smugglers. To do that, we decided we would tap the phone in the Lost Baggage Office, and hope to obtain enough information about the operation and when they would be making shipments. Therefore, the operations plan was sent to HQ OSI for action. A short time later, the plan came back approved. Once again, my friend Ed Linz helped get the operation approved.

The first phase of the operation was initiated a couple of days later. Thanks to a prior operation, JP had a good contact in the base telephone office. He had a tap put on the phone line for the Lost Baggage Office. Luckily, they only had one phone line in that office. The phone tap had been a simple jumper placed on the target line and cross-connected to a special line in our local OSI Office, where I had installed an automatically activated line pick-up and a recording device. For three days, JP and I had taken turns listening to the conversations that were recorded. If we did not listen "real time", to hear the conversations as they occurred, we would have to listen to hours of recordings after the fact. That was even more boring and meant if something important to the operation was heard on the tape recordings, the timetable for response might be past.

On the third day, in the afternoon, I was listening to the live conversation being recorded, and heard what I had been waiting for.

The conversation started with "Lost Baggage, Sgt. White."

A voice on the other end of the line said, "Whitey, Jonesy what's going on?"

"Aw you know Jonesy, Same Shit, Different Day. How goes the war? You been working on the railroad laying those Thai's?"

"Same as you, SSDD. Yeah, that railroad work is hard."

"You looking for some lost baggage?" White requested.

"Yeah, I think that three bags got shipped to yo' location by mistake. They belonged to a Lt. Joseph A. Arturo. He was scheduled to leave here yesterday, but got held back at the last minute due to some type of problem. Anyway, the bags got put on the plane first, and then we didn't have time to get them off before the flight departed."

"OK, I'll look around and see if I can find the bags. What do you want me to do with em?"

"Go ahead and send em back here. We don't know when the guy is going to leave now."

"Gotcha will do," said Sgt. White, and the conversation ended.

"Hey J P, get in here quick. I think we got something"

"I'm coming. What happened?" asked J P, as he quickly entered the room where we were listening and recording the phone tap.

"Sgt. White just got a weird call from someone named Jonesy in Thailand." I think they may have been sitting up a shipment."

After we both listened to the recorded conversation two times, we just did not feel confident the call had meant a shipment had just been arranged.

"You know, I really wish we were able to hear what Sgt. White and his lost baggage coworker were talking about after the telephone call," said J P.

"Yeah, I think we need to get permission to bug the phone in the Lost Baggage Office, instead of just a tap where we only hear the phone conversations," I replied.

"My thoughts exactly," said J P.

"I'll run it by Capt. Barker and Mike Miley to see what they think. After they listen to the tape recording, I think they will agree. And, I know I can get Ed Linz to approve the change in our Operational Plan," I said, already thinking about what I would need to do to get a bug into the Lost Baggage Office.

As I looked out of our office window that afternoon, I observed what I would come to believe to be one of the most profound classical differences between the eastern and western work conditions. Apparently, someone on Kadena Air Base had decided that the painted street lane markings on the main road into the base needed to be either changed or replaced. To the best of my knowledge, in the United States, if there was a requirement for that type of effort there would be a large, loud, lane-hogging machine that would be taking the painted stripes off the surface of the Macadam roadway. However, in the Orient, what I observed that day was about fifty little Mamasan's down on hands and knees, with hammers and chisels – chipping up the painted surface by hand. It was slow, tedious work in the hot sun, but I am sure that the job was done, and the Mamasan's were very happy to have the jobs.

CHAPTER 3

The decision to put a bug in the Lost Baggage Office had been made last Thursday, and today's phase of the operation was a direct result of the operation to date. Capt. Barker and Mike Miley had both agreed with the need to hear all of the conversations in the Lost Baggage Office after a suspicious telephone call like the one last week. Ed Linz had worked his magic and gotten the operational extension and bugging approved in short order. I had gotten the cooperation of the Noncommissioned Officer in Charge (NCOIC) of the telephone main frame at Kadena AB, who had helped us with the phone tap. The phone line for the Lost Baggage Department was shorted one morning and within an hour, the telephone maintenance office had received a call from the men in the targeted office.

"Hey man, the phone isn't working in the Lost Baggage Office at the air terminal," announced the frustrated voice at the other end of the line.

"Where're you calling from?" asked the NCOIC

"Well, I'm sure as hell not calling from my office," the frustrated voice replied.

"OK, OK, getting nasty won't get you anywhere. I'll put in a work order for your office and have someone out there tomorrow."

"Sorry, man, I didn't mean to be nasty, but this is a busy place, and I really need our phone. Please see if you can get someone out here this morning, I'm expecting an important call about some lost baggage."

"I'll see what I can do," said the NCOIC.

Therefore, here JP and I were pretending to be telephone maintenance people. As we got to the door of the Lost Baggage

147

Office, I looked at JP, gave him a thumbs up, and opened the door. As I stepped into the room, I immediately saw a long counter that stopped anyone from going any further into the room. Behind the counter, a man sat at a desk.

"Yes, can I help you?" a man with a nametag of White responded as JP and I entered the room.

"I'm Airman Douglas from the telephone maintenance office. I understand you're having a problem with your office telephone."

"You got it man," replied Sgt. White, "The damned thing just went dead this morning and hasn't worked since. I really appreciate you all being able to get out here this soon as I'm expecting an important call any time now. How soon do you think you can get it fixed?"

"Well, that depends upon what we find wrong," JP replied.

"Jake, if you want to look at the telephone instrument, I'll finish checking out the cable for this line," said JP.

"Sure," I said, as I turned to Sgt. White and asked, "Has anything happened to this telephone instrument lately?"

"No, I don't think so," replied Sgt. White. "What do you mean has anything happened to it?"

"Well, like has it been knocked off the desk or anything like that?"

"No, I don't think so"

"Wait a minute," said another person who had just entered the office area from a back door and overheard the question.

"Remember a few days ago when I accidently hit it with a suitcase I was moving, and it fell to the floor?" said the new person whose nametag said King.

"Oh yeah, that's right," stated White. "It didn't seem to hurt it none, but then it started acting funny after a few days."

"Ok, I'll check it out," I said.

"Hey, Jake, all of the wiring appears to be fine, and the junction box here on the wall checks out great," said J P.

I took the phone loose from its connector cable and plugged it into a telephone instrument analyzer I had with me. A few seconds later, after running a couple of tests on the phone, I announced,

"Ok, this thing has definitely got a problem. It appears that the primary receive circuit has a defective crossover network. Hey, Sgt. White, have you had problems hearing the people who are calling you recently?"

"Shit man, that damned thing, has had all kinds of problems. Sometimes, I can't hear the people, and sometimes they can't hear me. Then, this morning the son-of-a-bitch just went totally dead and quit working."

"Ok, JP, would you go out to the truck, and bring me one of the new phones? I think this one has seen its last day."

"Sure, Jake, I'll be right back with it."

Shortly after JP walked out of the door, I looked around the room at the racks of suitcases, parcels, and other miscellaneous boxes.

"I had no idea there were so many lost or misplaced items in an air terminal," I said in amazement.

"Oh yeah, man," Sgt. White said, "People are really a bunch of dumb asses. We gets all kinds of shit left on the conveyer belts out there. We have leftover crap almost every time a plane comes in here. Then, sometimes a little after a flight leaves or the next day or so, the stupid peoples come slinking in here looking to see if their shit is here."

"Man, I wouldn't have guessed that. My boss told me you really needed this phone fixed because you were expecting an important phone call today about some lost baggage."

"Yes, dat's right."

I thought to myself, *Sgt. White seemed to be a little bit nervous talking about that subject.*

"Well, no problem. We are going to have you fixed up here in a just a minute. I am sure a new phone is all you need. I know it's going to work better than that old one you had, and I think I can guarantee that!"

"I certainly hopes so," replied Sgt. White. "How the hell do you gets into the kind of work you do anyway? It looks like it would be very interesting."

"Well, it takes quite a bit of electronic training," I replied. "And you just wouldn't believe how interesting this job can be! There's always something different, and you end up catching a lot of problems."

About that time, JP came back into the room with the new phone. "Here you go, Jake. I'll bet this one will fix them right up."

He gave me a thumbs up signal, indicating he had called the telephone frame room and had them remove the short from the telephone line we were working on.

I connected the new phone to the cable and lifted the receiver off the hook switch. I smiled real big and said, "You've got dial tone. Let me call the telephone frame room to see how it's working. Hello, this is Jake. How does this phone seem to be? Working fine, that's great. Let me hang up, and you check it out then call me right back."

I hung up the telephone handset, and continued talking to JP. A couple of seconds later, the phone rang and I picked it up. "Everything seems to be OK, you hear me fine? Great."

"Well Sgt. White, I think you're back in business. I hope you get your important call today, and everything works just fine."

You just do not know how much I mean that friend, I thought.

"Thanks man for being able to come out this morning instead of tomorrow. I really appreciate you fixing us up."

"Believe us, it was our pleasure," stated JP, as he and I turned and walked out the door.

CHAPTER 4

A few minutes later, we were back at our listening post, and were thrilled at how well the telephone bug was working. Capt. Barker and Mike Miley were already there to hear the results of our efforts, and could not believe how well the bug was picking up conversations in the Lost Baggage Office.

"Just listen to that audio quality," said J P.

"Yeah, and we won't have any trouble recording on this Uher 4400 Recorder," I stated.

"Yes and with the backup recorder on line, we won't miss anything that goes on in that room."

Both Barker and Miley congratulated us on a job well done.

Capt. Barker asked me, "Do you think they had any idea what was going on, and what you two were actually doing?"

"Not at all," I replied. "They were so happy to get their phone working again I'm sure they never even thought anything was out of line."

"Ok, now comes the boring part, stated Miley. I love these operations, but this sitting and waiting for something to happen just drives me batty."

"Yeah, I know, but I've a feeling this one isn't going to take very long," I replied.

Therefore, we settled in for the long hours of listening to the live audio coming from the Lost Baggage Office. This was indeed the most boring portion of any operation. Listen to the audio. Change the tapes. In addition, make sure there was no recording time lost when audio recorders had to be switched at the end of the tapes. Keep the surveillance log current, and make entries for any and everything that happened. The audio tapes and surveillance logs were evidence, and therefore had to be properly marked, tagged and controlled at all times. Anytime there was any pertinent information obtained on tape, it had to be reviewed by the controlling case agent, and provided to the legal office for review.

On the day after the bug had been installed, at 10:00 am in the morning, JP was monitoring the tape recorder, and heard the following conversation.

"Lost Baggage," Sgt. White.

"White, Jonesy – you know those bags I called you about the other day? The three that belong to Lt. Arturo."

"Sure man, what about em?"

"Well, it turns out they didn't get out on the flight, we thought they did, after all. They left here later on a damned flight that was going to stop in Viet Nam first."

"How the hell did that happen?" asked Sgt. White. "It hasn't happened in two years. The flights always have come from Thailand straight to here. That's why we started using this route." Sgt. White was obviously very upset.

"I know man," said Jones. "What have we had twenty fo to thirty flights with no problems? I think there was some special baggage or VIP shit on that flight that caused it to have to stop in Nam."

"Yeah, but I don't think we ought to be discussing this on the damned telephone. You know that damned OSI has their fingers in everything over here." White was furious.

"Yeah OK, but you need to be on the lookout for those three suitcases. Even with a couple of hour's layover in Nam, they should still get to your location on tomorrow morning's flight."

"This could really screw up our whole thing!" White shouted. "After this flight, I think we better lay low for a while. Maybe a month or so. It isn't like we haven't made a bundle."

Jones was quite concerned now. "Man, I hate to stop a good thing especially when we gots it working so good."

"Yeah, I agree, but I think we'd better be safe than sorry. A month won't hurt us that bad. You don't leave Thailand for another three months, so hopefully you can set up someone else with your supplier there so we's can keep this golden pony trotting."

"OK, man," Jones said, "you just be sure to capture those three cases. They's a lot of good shit in em."

"Later bro, watch them hoes over there, you don't want to take anything home to your ol' lady."

"Don't worry Whitey – I haven't reached my PCOD yet."

"PCOD or not, you better keep that black snake in its cage."

"Yeah, Yeah – later bro," and Jones was gone.

White hung up the phone, and the audio immediately switched from a wiretap to a bug.

"Son of a Bitch King, why did this have to happen now?" It was Sgt. White's voice. "Only three mo' months left before Jones leaves Thailand. If we lay low for a month, that'll only leave us two months to milk this shit for all we can get out of it. I'll really have to push him to keep our supplier in the

loop. Besides, we gots all of these military and Okinawan dealers that we have to keep supplied. We can't just stop them cold. Hell, we'd have a damned riot here on this stinking island!"

"Jones just has to find someone who can keep this thing going. I've got close to three quarters of a million stashed, and I sure would like to make it a full million dollars before I quit and go back to the land of the big BX."

"Yeah man, I's got about that much stashed too," said Airman King. " I gets awfully nervous just having so much money stuck in my mattress!"

"I uses the same bank," said White. "If it's good enough fo' all of these little bow legged Okinawans it's good enough fo' me. Besides, my Okinawan ho' Yoshie, needs lots of things bought to keep her happy, and that makes getting to the 'bread' easy enough."

I walked into the listening post, and JP almost screamed at me. "We've got'em, we've got'em!"

"What happened, what are you screaming about?" I asked.

"What happened? I'll tell you what happened. Sit down and listen to what's on this tape, after I switch recorders," JP was so excited, he could hardly work.

After I listened to the tape, I decided to get Capt. Barker and Mike Miley to listen to it. When they came to the listening post, I could hardly control myself, and get the audio tape set up to listen to.

"Darn Jake, slow down," Barker told him.

"Sorry Capt.," I said. "They just handed everything to us on a platter. All we've got to do now is wait for the cases to come in, and for White to take them into his possession."

"What'd you mean Jake, what has happened?" asked Barker.

"Well, sir, sit down and listen to what we recorded today."

After hearing the tape recording, both Capt. Barker and Agent Miley were amazed that anyone would talk so much and that open, about such a sensitive matter. They had just compromised their whole operation.

"Wow," said Barker, "I wonder how many times they've been so stupid to talk so openly about exactly what they're doing?"

"Yeah, these guys are either so naïve or the stupidest idiots that I've ever heard of," replied Miley.

"So, Mike, what do you want to do with your case?" asked Barker.

"Well, sir, with them shutting down for a month, and the chance the whole operation may only go on for another two months after that, I say we bust them with this shipment, and stop this hemorrhaging of drugs into Okinawa."

"My sentiments exactly," stated Barker. "What'd you two think?" he asked JP and me.

"I can speak for both of us," said J P. "I think the time for action is now. However, we have thought of one other potential problem. How are we going to know what is going on in the Lost Baggage Office, after the three suitcases are taken there, and the guys have access to them without our knowledge?"

"Oh boy, I hadn't even thought of that," said Miley.

"Yeah, we thought not," said J P.

"Do you have any suggestions?" asked Barker.

"Well, sir, funny you should ask – of course we do! We think its past time to put at least one video camera into the Lost Baggage Office. Do you think we can commandeer a room in the air terminal to use as an observation post (OP)?"

"I don't see why not," said Barker. "One of my agents' wives is the building supervisor there. Her name is Michele Myer. I am sure we can get

her to provide us a room to use, especially after we brief her on the bad guys she's got working there."

"We already know of her opinion of those two guys in the Lost Baggage Office, believe me" said J P.

"How would you know that?" asked Miley.

"Well you see we kind of had a run in with her already. When we were pretending to be looking for the 'problem' with the target area phone, she was not happy we were in her building without her prior knowledge," said J P.

"That's alright," Miley said. "That's just her personality, you should meet her husband!"

"Well," replied J P, "all we need is a room, as close as possible to the target that we can lock from the inside, and not draw to much attention by using it."

CHAPTER 5

"**W**ith Mrs. Myer's help, we'll enter the target tonight after every one is gone from that area, and determine how many video cameras need to be installed to cover the room."

"How many do you think you'll need, and do you have them on hand?" Miley asked.

"Yeah, we have several in our inventory so we can handle these types of operations. From what I remember when we were in the target, I think we may get by with only one camera. However, I will need to see what's in the room behind the front counter area, and the shelves where they place the lost baggage. There must be a rear door or work area, as Airman King came from somewhere back there while we were checking their phone. Another potential problem we may have to deal with is whether or not the target has a false ceiling. I'll have to call our headquarters this afternoon though, and get their approval to expand the operational plan to include video, but that shouldn't be a problem."

"Jake, will you start checking out our video equipment, and complete an inventory of what we may need for cable, connectors, video tapes, etc.?"

"Sure J P," I replied.

"Capt. Barker, can you please check with Mrs. Myer about an available room and access into the target area tonight?"

"No problem J P."

Later that afternoon, Barker told JP there was a room we could use in the air terminal. It had been an office for someone who had retired, and it was no longer used. It was in the hallway opposite of the target area, and down a couple of rooms. The whole area in that part of the building had a dropped false ceiling, so access to the target area should be relatively easy.

"Alright then," said J P. "Tonight we'll put in one or two CCTV cameras per room to show as much of the inside of the target as possible. We will probably work the better part of the night, so Mike, you need to have another person read in on the operation, and in the OP early tomorrow morning, before the target is open."

"Have them bring plenty of water, something to eat, and an empty bottle for their personal relief. Unless we finish later than I figure, at least one of us will be there by 7:00 am to meet your person, and go over the operation of the equipment with them and show them how to mark the tapes as evidence, and complete the surveillance log."

"Everyone did a very good job today with all of the efforts and preparation," said Capt. Barker. "I hope everything goes well tomorrow, and we catch the bad guys and wrap this thing up. If we are able to bust those guys tomorrow, we will immediately notify the OSI Office in Thailand to bust the people on that end of the operation. Get some good rest tonight, and be ready to go tomorrow. Sorry Jake and J P; I know that won't happen for you two."

"Its ok, sir, we're used to these types of time tables and work", I said.

That night, at about 7:00 pm, Michele Myer let me and JP into the target area to determine where would be the best place to install the CCTV camera, or cameras, to get full coverage of the inside of the target. Once we made that determination, she gave us a key to the target area, and took us around to the room we would use as the OP and opened it up for us. She gave us a key to the room and left.

"Good luck," she said, as she departed.

"Thanks," said JP.

JP and I had quickly decided that we would only need two video cameras to cover the entire two-room target area. After looking in the front counter area, we were able to determine we should be able to conceal one of the Sony AVC 3200 CCTV cameras on top of a shelf that overlooked the target counter area and all of the front office space. There were a lot of unused boxes, etc. on that end of the shelf, and it was obvious nothing had been moved in quite a while. We would need a box that was at least eighteen inches long to fit the camera into, depending upon which lens we had to use with it. The 3200 camera was approximately thirteen inches long x four inches wide x four inches high, without a lens. We were able to place the camera inside one of the cardboard boxes, and cut a small hole, where there was some lettering, for the lens to view through.

It was perfect and it would be extremely unlikely anyone would have any reason to be up in that area for a few hours tomorrow, let alone need to look in the specific box that had contained a large amount of old records. We had moved those records to the OP Room. We felt very safe with the camera location.

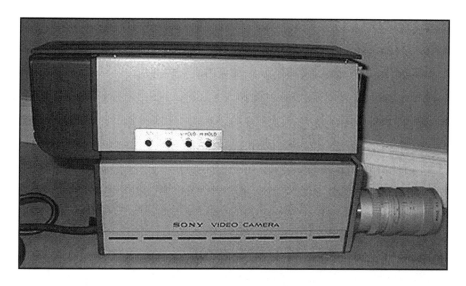

Sony AVC 3200 Video Camera (with attached video monitor). In our surveillance operations, the monitor would not have been used. Photo Courtesy of Ed Sharpe/SMECC

However, the camera in the second room would prove to be harder. There was a rear door to the back of the target area, and a large table that items could be placed on. There was no easy place in that area to install the second camera.

Therefore, as we often had to do, we would install the camera above the false ceiling, and make a small hole in the ceiling tile to allow a pinhole lens to "see through" the acoustic ceiling tile. This required some type of mounting hardware to mount the camera at an approximate forty-five degree angle. Looking through the ceiling with a pinhole lens was a common practice, and one, which amazingly was almost never observed by anyone in a target area. Even if the personnel in the target area did notice the hole, they almost never remembered whether the hole was new or if it had been there all along.

It took us about six hours to install the two video cameras, and run the cables from the target area, over the false ceiling tiles and to the OP room. While I was crawling around in the false ceiling, I slipped and put my hand through one of the acoustic tiles. I was lucky I did not fall through the ceiling and hurt myself, but it meant we had to quickly look around, and find an extra ceiling tile.

We were lucky enough to find several tiles hidden away in a janitor's closet. Once we got the cables laid above the false ceilings, we hooked the cables to two Sony AV 3650 Video Recorders, and connected two Sony video monitors to the recorders. Once the monitors were installed, we could make the final adjustments to the video cameras to get the best view needed of the target area. Finally, we placed new video tapes on the recording machines, zeroed the tape counters, completed the initial entries in the surveillance log concerning the installation and made sure everything was ready for tomorrow morning. We took several still photographs of the target area, the installation of the CCTV cameras and wiring and the OP for my report. We had already made sure everything in the target area was exactly as we had found it, and we had not left anything out of place.

Overall, it had been a short installation. That was mainly due to the fact the OP was so close to the target.

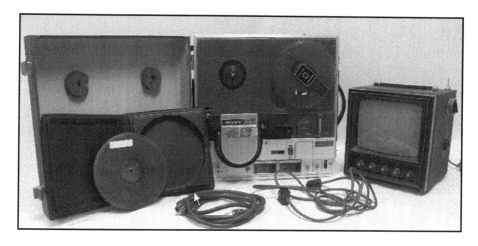

Sony AV 3650 Video Recorder, shown with a 12" Video Monitor Photo Courtesy of Ed Sharpe/SMECC

Earlier the previous day, Capt. Barker had asked J P, Miley and me how we thought the operation would be able to be completed.

"Well, sir," I replied "my idea is to see if we can determine if OSI has a trusted source in the Air Terminal or the Aircraft Maintenance Squadron at Ton Son Hut Air Force Base in Saigon. If we can get someone to verify those three suitcases are in fact on that aircraft, and exactly what they look like, then we just set up a surveillance in the Air Terminal here and watch for the suitcases to arrive."

"As soon as they do, and are taken to the Lost Baggage Office, and Sgt. White or his helper make any attempt to open the suitcases and leave the area with the drugs we simply make our bust."

"That sounds like a good thought," replied Mike Miley. "I have a close friend who works in the Security Police at Ton Son Hut. I bet he'd have a

thought on how we can accomplish our goal of checking on those three suitcases. I'll call him right now on the secure phone, and see what he has to say."

"Alright, please do that," asked Capt. Barker. "Be sure to tell him of the sensitivity of the matter, and the absolute need not to compromise the operation or even remotely draw undue attention to those suitcases. We've no idea at this point if the smuggling operation has anyone affiliated with it in Saigon."

"Yes, sir, I'll get right on it," replied Miley.

"That's one good thing about working with the military," I stated. "The networking almost always works out well for operations such as this."

"That's true Jake, we do have some extra advantages in the military that come in very handy sometimes," said Miley.

"JP and I will continue to monitor the audio for anything else that might be significant," I advised.

A couple of hours later, Miley returned to the listening post with Barker.

"Anything else happened?" asked Mike.

"No, it's been pretty quiet so far," replied J P. "What were you able to find out?"

"Well, my friend didn't have anyone he trusted enough to do the job, because of the sensitivity. However, Ton Son Hut had a minor attack shortly before I called him, and due to his response teams being deployed to protect the airfield and the aircraft parked on the ramps, my friend had to conduct a patrol of the airfield and ramp areas. He was able to direct some of his people to check all aircraft parked on the ramp to make sure no one got into them, and there was no damage to any of them. He had already been able to determine which C-130 had come in from Thailand within the past twenty-four hours. So, he made sure he was the person who checked out that aircraft."

There are three dark gray Samsonite suitcases, all marked as belonging to a Lt. Joseph A. Arturo on that plane."

"Bingo," I said. "But that makes them blend in with other common suitcases, which could be a problem, but let's just hope there aren't too many other dark gray Samsonite cases on that flight. The thing we'll be looking for is simply at least three suitcases that fit the description."

"I've had time to plan what I want for the surveillance tomorrow," stated Mike Miley. "I've got a contact in the Air Terminal, and have been able to determine a flight from Ton Son Hut is scheduled to arrive tomorrow at 10:00 am. I will be scheduled for a flight out of Kadena tomorrow at 12:00 noon, so I'll be inside the terminal as if I'm waiting on my flight. I will have one of my Agents in the observation post with Jake and J P. There'll be another one of my agents in the Air Control Tower, under the guise of a potential threat to the flight line, so he can tell us exactly when the aircraft from Saigon arrives and the baggage is unloaded."

Mike continued, "Once we know the baggage is in the receiving area, I'll be able to monitor it, and let the observation post know when Sgt. White or his partner has picked up the three suitcases. The observation post will then monitor what is going on in the target area, and Capt. Barker will monitor the audio from the bug in the target. We want to wait until the suspects open the three suitcases, and move the stuff out of the target area before we move in for an arrest. We will all have two-way communications, and the call sign for tomorrow will be "Mary."

"Mary 1 will be me," Mike said. The person in the Control Tower will be Mary 2, the OP will be Mary 3, and Capt. Barker, monitoring the bug for audio, will be Mary 4. If we need any more radios they'll just pick up the next number."

"That sounds very good to me," said Barker.

"Alright, JP, and I will continue to monitor the audio to make sure nothing happens to mess up the plan," I said.

"OK, I think we're ready for tomorrow", said Miley.

CHAPTER 6

The next morning, JP and I were both in the OP by 6:45 am. We were both dressed in our "undercover" fatigues, in case we happened to run into either of the two men in the target area, before the operation began. At 7:00 am, OSI Agent Richard Bock knocked on the door, and when allowed into the OP, said that Mike Miley had sent him.

"Great, said J P. Let me show you what we have going and how things work. Even though there are two of us technical agents here, we never know what is going to happen, and one of us may have to leave the OP for some reason. Therefore, it's important you not only know what we're doing and how to operate the equipment, but you need to feel comfortable about using the equipment, changing the video tapes and making entries in the surveillance log."

Richard was amazed at the quality of the video pictures of the target area, especially when told where and how the two cameras were installed. He was given thorough training on how to operate everything.

At approximately 7:30 am, Sgt. White entered the target area to start his workday. Soon afterwards, Airman King arrived. They were both oblivious of the two camera locations, and carried on with their apparent normal routines.

At 10:00 am, there was an announcement on the Air Terminal Public Address System that a C-130 has just arrived from Saigon, Viet Nam and should be in front of the terminal shortly.

Everyone had been waiting for that queue. I used my Motorola HT220 Radio to verify that everyone was in place, and ready for the expected action. I got a reply everyone was there and ready however, Miley advised there was a need for one other person to be in a new location to better observe the rear of the C-130, because of the way it had been parked on the ramp. I advised I could cover that if there was no one else available. Miley requested me to do that.

"Sure, I can do it now that we have Richard here to help J P. Where do you want me to go?"

"There's a storage building directly behind the rear of the C-130. You should have a great view of the plane from there," replied Miley.

"Roger that, I'm on my way."

As I exited the OP and started down the hall towards the ramp area, I heard a voice behind me say:

"Airman Douglas, are you still working on telephones in this building?"

I turned around to see Airman King coming down the hall behind me. My heart jumped up into my throat for a second, and my pulse skyrocketed. I immediately regained my composure and was able to smile and say.

"Hey, Airman King, how's it going? Yeah, we had another call about some telephone troubles in this building, and they wanted us to take out some instruments that had been used in that office I just came out of."

"Yeah, that dude retired recently I heard," said King.

" Where're you headed?" I asked.

"Oh, I got's to go to the C-130 that just landed to hep with the baggage"

"Alright man, I'll see you later," I said as I watched Airman King stroll on down the hall and out towards the aircraft.

"Mike, I'm not going to be able to get out to the rear of the airplane after all. I just ran into Airman King as I was coming out of the OP. He's going out to the airplane, and there's no way I can get out to that building without him seeing me." I said on the radio.

"That's OK Jake; I think we'll be able to identify the material if it comes off the plane. You'd better get back into the OP and stay low."

"Roger that."

A few minutes later, "Mary 2" notified everyone an Airman and a cart with a bunch of baggage had just departed the C-130 and was moving towards the terminal building. A couple of seconds later, the report came that there were at least two gray suitcases on the cart.

Shortly after that, "Mary 1" announced there were in fact three dark gray Samsonite suitcases on the cart, and all the baggage was being off loaded and placed on the conveyor belt. There were several people waiting for their bags, and as the baggage came around the conveyer people were claiming their bags.

After about fifteen minutes, an announcement was made over the intercom, that any remaining baggage from the Saigon flight would be available in the Lost Baggage Office in about a half hour. At that point, Airman King was observed by "Mary 1" taking the three Samsonite bags, on a small dolly, to the target area.

"Mary 1 to all players, the items are being taken to the target. Be ready to observe and react."

Shortly after that notice, J P, Richard and I observed the three bags being brought into the rear door of the target, by Airman King. He placed the bags onto the table in the rear section of the office, and went to the front section and was observed talking to Sgt. White.

At that moment, Mary 4 announced White & King were talking about what they wanted to do with the stuff. White was saying they'd wait a few minutes until increased activity in the terminal slowed down. Then, they'd put their "closed" sign on the front door. After that, they would open the cases, put some of the drugs into their personal bags and one at a time would take the stuff to their cars. They'd meet at White's house that night to decide what to do with the stuff.

"Mary 1 to all players, we'll watch and wait until both Subjects have loaded their personal bags and departed the target. If they depart at separate times, I will discretely follow the first to leave and call for back up to join me at a distance until I get the word the second suspect has been arrested. By the way, Jake and J P, I think you two should remain in the OP and let Agent Bock arrest the second Subject. I will then arrest the one I'm following. Everyone copy?"

"Mary 2 copy."

"Mary 3 copy."

"Mary 4 copy."

At approximately, 11: 45 am, Sgt. White and Airman King both went to the rear of the target area, and loaded the stuff from the three Samsonite cases into their personal bags. It was obvious to the OP crew the two bags being used to transport the stuff were fairly large canvas type duffel bags and were heavy.

At 12:00 pm, Sgt. White departed the target area through the rear door with his bag, and went out to his personal vehicle. As he drove away, Mike Miley was in pursuit at a discreet distance.

At 12:15 pm, after placing the closed sign on the front door of the Lost Baggage Office, Airman King also departed the target through the rear door and went to his car. He opened the trunk, and placed his duffle bag in it and closed the trunk lid. As he got into his personal car, and before he could start it, he was arrested by Agent Bock.

"Mary 5 to all Mary's, suspect #2 is in the bag, so to speak."

"Mary 1 roger. Back up, please join me, and stop suspect #1 for the arrest."

A few minutes later, everyone heard:

"This is Mary 1. Suspect #1 is in the bag."

"Mary 1 to Mary 3."

"Mary 3 here."

"Close up shop, remove your equipment and get out of dodge."

"Copy that."

A few hours later, after JP and I had removed all of the equipment, and cleaned up the two rooms, we met Mike Miley in the OSI Headquarters.

"How're things going?" asked J P.

"Well, when we opened the two duffle bags, we ended up with a total of forty kilos of hashish and ten grams of cocaine. However, as usual, both suspects are stating they do not know how the stuff got into the trunk of their cars. How soon can you set up a recorder and monitor to show them their 'moment of fame'?" Miley asked.

"Wow, that's a pretty respectable haul. We'll have it set up in fifteen minutes", I said.

Miley went back to interrogating Sgt. White.

"Sgt. White, I am going to ask you one more time, where'd you get the drugs we found in the trunk of your car?"

"Screw you pig; I don't have any idea what you're talking about!"

Miley had moved the interrogation to another room from where he had

started talking to Sgt. White. There was not much in the new room. A small table and two chairs, one on each side of the table. In the corner of the room, there was another small table, with a sheet covering several items.

Miley stepped over to the entry door and opened it. He motioned for someone to enter, turned to Sgt. White, and said:

"Sgt. White, I'd like for you to meet someone. I think you two have met previously. This is Airman Douglas or should I say, Special Agent Jake Douglas from the OSI."

White's face got a definite show of concern.

"I think Mr. Douglas has something to show you that you'll find very interesting. Go ahead Jake."

As I took the sheet off the equipment that had been setting on the second table in the room, it revealed a video monitor and a video recorder. As I pushed the "play" button on the recorder, a picture came into focus on the monitor screen. The view was of the interior of the front of the Lost Baggage Office and Sgt. White sitting at his desk.

Sgt. White immediately said, "Hey that's my office and that's me."

Then his mouth dropped open and he lost all expression as the view changed to him and Airman King opening the three dark gray Samsonite suitcases and begin loading their contents into the canvas duffle bags.

"Oh Shit!" He said. "You Pigs done got me for sure. I guess you've already caught Airman King, huh?"

"Yes," Mike Miley replied. He had about the same thing to say as you just did!"

The next day, after making sure, all of the video and audio tapes from the operation were properly marked as evidence and stored, we had made the necessary excerpts from the audio and video tapes to use in the trial, JP, and I cleaned our equipment for storage until the next time we would need it. This was the dreary part of the job that always accompanied the end of an operation.

Sgt. White and Airman King were both incarcerated pending their trial. Upon additional questioning, Airman King was given the promise of a lighter sentence if he cooperated by naming the accomplices who were involved in the Thailand end of the drug smuggling. He was reluctant, but when presented the probability of a long sentence, he assisted by naming the two Air Force personnel who had worked with him and Sgt. White. The next day, Sgt. Jones and his assistant were arrested in Thailand. The whole drug operation had been broken. After the primary players had been arrested and jailed, the OSI, with the cooperation of the local Okinawan Police had raided the off-base homes of Sgt. White and Airman King. In addition to some left over drugs, one and a half million dollars in U.S. currency was found in the mattresses of both Airmen. All of this was secured as evidence for their trial. At the same time, OSI agents and their counterparts in the Thailand Police raided the homes of Sgt. Jones and his accomplice in Thailand, with approximately the same results.

Several months later, we got the results of the trial of Sgt. White and Airman King, in addition to their accomplices in Thailand.

They had all received the maximum sentence available for the smuggling of drugs, the illegal use of U.S. military aircraft and various other charges that could be used to prosecute them. They would be spending a large portion of the next part of their lives in prison.

OPERATION III

Location: Anderson AFB, Guam

Allegation: Smuggling Expensive Private Contraband
via U.S. Military Aircraft

CHAPTER 1

We had just barely gotten all of the equipment cleaned and put away from our drug case, when Capt. Gary Tarper (the OSI District 41TSD Chief and my boss) called me into his office.

"What's up boss?" I said.

"I just got a call from OSI Headquarters, they have another operation that needs done on a short notice."

"Oh, ok is this one going to JP?"

"It could; however, it is in a place that you are familiar with so I thought that you might be interested in the job."

"Would that be Guam?" I asked.

"Yes it is Jake. I know that you still are suffering some bad memories of that location, but the job is only a three-day trip so you could get in and out quickly and get the job done. Additionally, you have worked with Capt. Byer over there, and have a good rapport with him, so that may help the operation."

"I just don't know if I can take going back there so soon Captain. There are so many memories that still haunt me."

"Well, we have a day or two to decide who goes, but it is a job that we have to get done soon."

"Can I ask what the job is, sir?"

"Of course. What I know at this point is that there will be a shipment of some suitcases, full of very expensive gold plated cigarette lighters, that are expected to be on a military aircraft, called the 'Guam Flyer' that will be going from Hong Kong to Japan. The job is to intercept the suitcases, pick the locks on each one, survey the contents of the suitcases and take photos of everything. Apparently, the suitcases can be taken off of the aircraft for a limited time frame and then returned, as the aircraft will have to RON (remain overnight) on Guam, for crew rest, before going on to Japan."

"Really, sir, cigarette lighters (I said with a snicker)? Don't we have anything more important to do than run some two-bit operation on some suitcases full of cigarette lighters?"

"I know it sounds pretty mundane Jake and hardly worth our effort; however, I have been told that the Air Force people involved with this caper have been doing it for quite some time. It involves many gold and silver items other than lighters, to include coins and bars, and they have made a huge amount of money getting the items to Japan to be sold on the black market there. Besides, they are using military aircraft to conduct their illegal operation."

"Ok, sir, let me think about it for a while this afternoon, and I will give you an answer today."

"Sure Jake, just let me know so we can get the flight reservations made."

I sat in the office that afternoon, and reminisced over the events that had occurred on Guam and the reason that I was now stationed and working in Okinawa. I was actually sorry that Okinawa had been given responsibility for any technical support needed on Guam. I finally decided that my prior unfortunate events just could not be allowed to interfere with my personal feelings, and any work that may need to be accomplished on Guam. It was our responsibility, and I would not be able to avoid going there eventually.

Later that afternoon, I told Capt. Tarper that I would take the job.

"Good Jake, I had hoped it might assist you to get over your feelings.

You need to call the base operations and let them know that you will be the one traveling to Guam. In addition, you need to call Ed Linz at Headquarters and let him know that you will be taking this assignment. Then you should call the OSI office at Yokota Air Base in Japan to coordinate with the technical office there."

"Yes, sir, right away."

"Hello Slick, this is Jake. How is life treating you these days?"

"Well Well, to what do I owe the pleasure of speaking to the infamous Jake Douglas?"

"That's because I am going to be the one going to Guam for the suitcase caper."

"Oh crap Jake, I didn't think they would ask you to do this case."

"Capt. Tarper gave me the choice and the freedom to accept the job or not. Since I am familiar with Capt. Byer and the layout over there, it was just easier for me to do it rather than one of the other guys. Besides, I decided that I really need to get that terrible event behind me as I will obviously be doing work on Guam from now on."

"Yeah, I guess you are right. Are you sure that you are up to it so soon though?"

"Yes, it has to be done," I said.

"OK, well I now know that the 'Guam Flyer' that is supposed to be carrying the suitcases will be leaving Hong Kong in three days and will be doing a RON on Guam that night. There should be three or four suitcases, and they are reportedly going to be dark gray Samsonite cases. Each suitcase should contain approximately two hundred Dunhill gold plated cigarette lighters. Since, this entire operation will only be using military aircraft, and will only be conducted on a military base it will be easy to bring the cases to the Anderson AFB, OSI Office for a few hours and then returned to the aircraft later. Therefore, you should have plenty of time to open the cases, survey and list the contents, and photograph all of the contents of each suitcase. Do you have any questions for me about this matter?"

"Do you still need me to submit an operational plan for this one?" I asked.

"Yes, unfortunately I do since I still need to go through the formality of getting the Headquarters Technical Service Directorate and the Criminal Service Directorate approvals for the operation."

"Alright, I will have that in to you today."

"Thanks ol' buddy and good luck with the trip and your demons."

"As always, Ed, I appreciate your concerns."

After speaking to Ed, I called Kadena Base Operations to set-up a flight to Guam.

"Base Operations, this is an unsecure line, this is Sgt. Green may I help you please?"

"Yes Sgt. Green, this is Special Agent Jake Douglas with OSI. I need to schedule a flight to Anderson AFB, Guam tomorrow or the next day."

"You are in luck, sir; we have a MAC Contract flight leaving day after tomorrow at 1000 hours. Would you be able to make that flight?"

"Yes I can be ready for that flight, and it would be just perfect," I replied.

"Fine then, just be here forty-five minutes early to sign-up for the flight, and to check in any luggage you might have."

"Great, thank you Sgt. Green, for your assistance."

"No problem, sir, I'll see you day after tomorrow."

Next, I had to call Capt. Byer to let him know that I would be the one coming to do the cigarette lighter case. I would need him to arrange to have the suitcases discreetly off loaded from the aircraft, and taken to the OSI Office on the evening they arrived. They would be ready for return to the aircraft early the next morning. In addition, if possible I would like to depart Anderson the day after I completed the job, for my return to Okinawa.

"Hello, this is Special Agent Byer, may I help you please?"

"Hello Shaun, this is Jake, can you talk for a minute?"

"Hey Jake, how are you doing? Sure, I can talk what can I do for you?"

"Well, I am going to be the one coming over to help you with the cigarette lighter case."

"Darn Jake, I didn't expect it to be you. Can't anyone else come over instead?"

"Sure there are a couple of other guys that could do it, but since I know you and the layout there I volunteered. Besides, I need to face my demons and get it over with."

"I can understand that, but it's just so soon. You will still see visible remnants of the crash – and that may be hard for you to take."

"I'm sure it will be, but maybe it will be easier for me to put it all together and get it behind me."

"Alright, what can I do for you on this end?" Shaun asked.

"I have already spoken to Ed Linz and we now know there should be three or four dark gray suitcases coming your way in three days, with the items in them. I need you to arrange to get the suitcases secretly brought to your office so that I can work on them in private. I will arrive on Anderson day after tomorrow in the afternoon. The Guam Flyer should arrive at your location the following evening. Therefore, I will work for as long as it takes that night, and you will be able to get the suitcases back onto the aircraft early the next morning. Can you please make reservations for a Visiting Officers Quarters room, and for my return flight back to Okinawa as soon as possible after I finish the work?"

"Sure I will take care of everything for you."

"Thanks for your help, I'll see you in two days."

"Sure Jake, have a good flight over."

So now, all I had left to do was get together anything that I would want to take with me for the job, submit an operations plan to Ed for approval and call the OSI Office at Yokota Air Base, Japan.

I completed the operations plan first, since I had to send it to Ed, and time was short for a turn around on the approval. The plan was easy as all it entailed was for me to fly to Guam; meet with Capt. Byer; open the suitcases when they were brought to the OSI Office; survey, photo and document the contents; and then return to Okinawa.

As far as what I needed to take to Guam with me, that was easy. Just some basic lock picks and a decent camera. I chose to take a Nikon 33mm camera with a close-up capability.

Now, for the call to the OSI District 46 Technical Office at Yokota Air Base.

"Hello, technical services, this is Special Agent Jimmy Leitz may I help you please?"

"Yes, Jimmy, this is Special Agent Jake Douglas at OSI District 41 TSD. I am calling to talk to someone about the scheduled work on Guam."

"Well, you have reached the right person. I am the Special Agent in charge of that job. Actually Howard Foote and I are working that case."

"Great, all I need to tell you is that I have been briefed by Ed Linz, and I will be the one traveling to Guam for the job. Do you have any additional information or changes for me?"

"No everything is on schedule as far as we know. When are you traveling?"

"Day after tomorrow. I'll arrive that afternoon," I said.

"Ok, if we hear anything different before you leave I'll call you at DO 41; otherwise I will leave a message with someone on Guam."

"Great, I'll let you know how things went before I leave Guam. I plan to make a complete inventory of the contents and take photos too. I will send you a copy of everything I find on the next available flight."

"Alright Jake, thanks for the heads up. Hope you have a good trip."

"Yeah, thanks also Jimmy. So long.

"So I just had to wait for a couple of days – and live with my demons!"

CHAPTER 2

While the flight from Okinawa was not very long, it seemed to take forever – as I tried to quiet my demons and get the past out of my mind. The aircraft was full of military personnel and their dependents. They were mostly returning to assignments back in the good ol' USA, and therefore they were happy and rather loud. I had the opportunity to talk to a few people who were sitting around me, and was filled-in on their up-coming assignments. If it was a place that I had been, they wanted to know everything I knew about the place and the military base. The one thing that helped my nerves somewhat was that there was a movie shown, after an hour or so into the flight.

When the flight attendant announced that we were starting our decent towards Guam and should be arriving there within about twenty minutes, all of my demons came flooding back into my mind. What the heck was I doing on this trip? Was I a complete idiot for even taking this job? I hoped that I could keep my emotions in check when I stepped off the aircraft.

I was still struggling with my thoughts and fears, when the flight attendant again announced that we were only minutes from landing and everyone needed to return all of their trash, place their seatbacks in the up-right position and close any food trays that may still be down. I felt a sudden rush of emotions, and knew that I had to try harder to remain as calm as possible.

As we made our final approach and was nearing the end of the runway, I could not keep myself from looking out of the window next to me. All of a sudden, I saw a deep gash in the grass area located between the main runway and the taxi apron. It seemed to be so deep and stretched away and towards the main parking ramp near the air terminal. At that same time, I heard someone near me ask what might have caused it. I knew immediately exactly, what had caused the deep scar, and I could not hold back my emotions any longer. Although I cried, I was able to keep it somewhat under control, and remained outwardly as calm as possible. Luckily, I had carried a handkerchief for exactly this expected event and was able to feign something like an allergy attack or cold so that most of the people around me could not tell for sure what was wrong.

I felt a little embarrassed about my wet and very likely red eyes, but was relatively sure no one knew why I was having a problem. Again, luckily for me, that hussle-bussle of everyone trying to get off of the plane for the required re-fueling and lay-over meant that most people were fairly preoccupied with getting their personnel belonging together to exit the plane. I was able to get into the main terminal, and get to a restroom to freshen-up before I had to retrieve my one checked suitcase. On the way from the plane to the terminal though, I could not help but observe the scars on the parking ramp and the burned remains of what I knew had been the temporary trailers where Melinda had been working on that fateful afternoon. By the time I actually got into the restroom, I had to sit in one of the stalls for quite a few minutes.

After what seemed to be a very long time, I was able to regain my composure, washed my face, and straightened up my clothes. As I walked out to the area to reclaim my luggage, I heard someone that sounded far away say, "Hello Jake, I figured that you might have needed to go to the men's room."

I looked up to see Shaun Beyer standing by the luggage return beltway.

"Hello Shaun, thanks very much for meeting me."

"Glad to do it Jake, and to see you again. How was the flight?"

"It wasn't really all that bad – until we got near the end of the runway and I saw that long deep scar. It was hard to hold it together I must admit."

"I'm sure it was Jake. Let's get your stuff, and get away from this part of the base. My wife has dinner planned, so that you can get away from everything and relax this evening."

"Darn, you guys didn't have to do that, but I assure you that I do appreciate it. Do you think I should go by the VOQ and sign-in before we go to your place?"

"No, I have already checked you in, and you have a room assigned so you are in good shape."

As we rolled into Shaun's on-base quarters driveway, I noticed the curtain in the front window gently move back into place. I guessed that Shaun's wife had been watching out the window for our arrival.

As we entered the house, Shaun said, "Honey, this is Jake Douglas that I have told you about. Jake, this is my wife Jaime."

"Hello Jaime, it is very nice to meet you," I said. "I certainly appreciate you making dinner this evening and having me over."

"It is my pleasure, and I am very glad to meet you after all I have heard about you. Would you care for anything to drink before dinner?"

"Would you happen to have any Jack Daniels?" I asked

"Why, yes we do actually."

"Great, I'll take a JD and water – in a tall glass please"

"Honey, would you like your usual Johnnie Walker on the rocks?"

"Yes please," Shaun said.

We sat and visited for a few minutes and drank our drinks.

"I know it may be out of place, but I was truly sorry to hear of your loss, and I told Shaun that it must be extremely difficult for you to return to the island so soon."

"Thanks Jaime, I appreciate your concern – and yes it was hard to return here, but I will be responsible for work here so I felt it was best to face it now rather than later."

After a wonderful dinner and dessert, we visited for a while longer, and then I asked Shaun to take me to the VOQ, as I was tired.

"Thank you both for a pleasant, relaxing evening and your hospitality."

"Jake, you are welcome here anytime you are on the island," Jaime said.

"Thanks, it was my pleasure to meet you Jaime."

As Shaun and I walked outside I asked, "Shaun, do you know what time the Guam Flyer is supposed to arrive tomorrow evening?"

"Yes, it should get here at around 6:00 pm."

"OK, when do you expect to have the suitcases in your office?"

"I had figured that we should allow the plane crew to depart the flight line, and give it another hour or so before we attempt to remove the suitcases from the plane. That would probably make it around 7:30 or 8:00 pm. What if we plan for you to arrive at the office at say 8:30 pm?"

"That sounds good to me. Will you still be there or do you want to give me a key?"

"I'll be at the office when you get there."

"OK, I'll see you tomorrow evening. Thanks again for tonight."

"You're welcome, take care Jake."

CHAPTER 3

At 8:30 pm, I arrived at the OSI Office. Shaun was there and let me in the door.

"Good evening Jake, how did your day go?"

"It was alright, I said. I went over to the golf course, hit a bucket of balls, and played nine holes. Although it was somewhat difficult, it managed to let me get rid of my demons and I actually enjoyed it."

"Good, well I have three Samsonite suitcases for you to work your magic on. Based upon your previous experiences here, that shouldn't be too difficult for you," he said as he grinned.

"Alright, I guess I need to get to work in case there is more to it than there should be. After all, we have a time table to keep on this matter."

"OK then, I'll see you tomorrow Jake."

First, I placed rubber gloves on my hands. Then, I carefully placed each one of the three suitcases on the top of a desk, in turn, and took photos of the exterior of each case and of any distinguishing marks and/or damage.

Next, I took a typical Samsonite suitcase key that I had with me and tried it on one of the locks of the last suitcase I had placed on a desk. Not to my surprise, the key turned in the lock and after opening the second lock, I opened the lid to the suitcase. There in front of me were a very large number of small expensive looking boxes. I guessed there were probably one to two hundred of them in the suitcase. I took a photo of the open suitcase and its contents. I carefully opened one of the boxes, and found a beautiful gold plated Dunhill Cigarette Lighter. After inspecting the lighter, I saw that it had an individual serial number engraved on the bottom. Therefore, now I knew that I had a way to identify each lighter. I would photograph each small box unopened, then photograph each box opened with the lighter in it, next I would take a photo of the bottom of each lighter, and then I would make a list of the type of each lighter as well as its serial number. That would give a detailed description of the contents of each of the three suitcases and photos to verify it all.

The overall process took me seven hours to complete. After making sure that, the contents of each suitcase were back inside, in the proper order and everything looked as it had when I opened them, I locked all three suitcases and placed them in Lt. Byer's office. I also left him the rolls of film and the written lists of the contents of each suitcase. He was scheduled to get the cases back on board the aircraft by 5:00 am that morning.

At 9:30 am the next morning, I went to the OSI Office and spoke to Lt. Byer.

"Good Morning Jake, you look a little ragged," Shaun said.

"Yes, I didn't get out of here until after 3:30 am this morning. Each one of those lighters was individually serial numbered, which slowed me down some."

"Well, the suitcases were back on board the aircraft by 5:00 am and I saw the Guam Flyer depart Anderson AFB at about 8:45 today. Thanks very much, again, for your excellent work and efforts. I will see to it that all of your photos and documentation are on the next flight to Japan so our guys up there will have the evidence they need to bust this operation."

"Thanks a lot. Can I use your encrypted phone to call DO 46 and let them know what I found?"

"Certainly, do you need me to leave the room?"

"No that is not necessary at all."

After two rings, someone answered the encrypted phone in the DO 46 Office. "Yes, this is Special Agent Jake Douglas calling for Jimmy Leitz, please."

"Sure, it will take me a couple of minutes to get him, please hold on" the voice said.

"Jimmy Leitz here, can I help you please?"

"Jimmy, this is Jake. I just wanted to let you know that I was able to go through the three suitcases last night. There were about two hundred items in each suitcase. They were all in individual boxes, with individual serial numbers on the bottom of each item. I took a photo of the exterior of each case, of each case opened, of each box unopened, each box opened and each serial number. You should have all of the information you could possibly need for evidence in this operation."

"Great Jake, it sounds like you did an excellent job. You must have had a long night huh? Did you have any problems getting the suitcases off of the aircraft and back on?"

"No, Capt. Beyer handled all of that for me and did a great job. I'm sure there were no reasons for anyone to suspect anything at all about the work on the suitcases."

"OK, we will handle the operation from here. Thanks for your assistance, and tell Capt. Beyer of our appreciation also."

"Will do," I said. "If you get time later, call me in Okinawa and let me know what happened on your end."

"I will, I promise. Take care."

I told Capt. Beyer of the appreciation of the DO 46 people and that we should eventually hear about how things went on their end.

"Well, my flight back to Okinawa leaves at 11:00 am, as you know, so I guess that I should get down to the air terminal and check-in. Thanks again for your efforts to make this trip as easy and comfortable as possible. I will see you on the next trip back this way, whenever that may be."

As my aircraft taxied towards the runway, and then started its takeoff roll, I glanced out the window and once again saw the remnants of the terrible accident that had taken the lives of that BUFF crew – and the woman that I loved and still thought of more often than I wanted to. I knew that Guam would continue to haunt me for some time to come.

A month later, I heard from Jimmy Leitz that all personnel associated with the smuggling operation in both Japan and Hong Kong had been caught and prosecuted and that operation would no longer be working.

OPERATION IV

Location: Clark Air Base, Philippines
Allegation: Theft of U.S. Government Paychecks from
the U.S. Mail

CHAPTER 1

In the spring of 1973, OSI Headquarters made the decision to move the Technical Services Division from OSI District 41 on Kadena AB, Okinawa to OSI District 42 on Clark AB, Philippines. The reason for this decision was based upon the fact Okinawa was reverted to Japan, and there was a large TSD in Japan that could cover Okinawa. In addition, a lot of the technical support mission for the personnel in Okinawa was actually located in the Philippines. With the move of the TSD, the technical personnel in the Philippines would continue to cover Taiwan and Guam.

Another significant change would also take place with the transfer of the TSD. Three of the four technical personnel who were assigned to Okinawa were close enough to their normal return date to the U.S., so it was decided to go ahead and allow them to rotate back to stateside assignments. That left me to transfer to the Philippines, and start setting up a new TSD. Since a significant level of work was going to be lost, with the transfer of the TSD from Okinawa, it was also decided the new TSD in the Philippines would only require three technical personnel. So, the two new personnel would be a captain and a master sergeant, with me now being a technical sergeant.

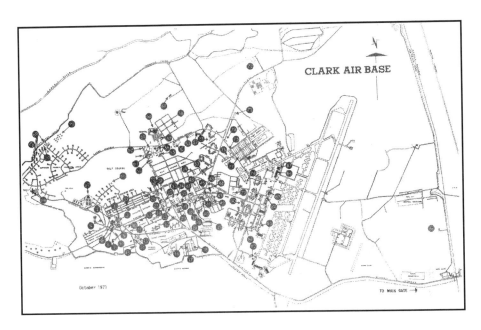

Clark Air Base Map circa 1971 Courtesy of U.S. Air Force

Clark Air Base Philippines Main Gate circa 1974 courtesy of U.S. Air Force

Therefore, in early July 1973, after being in Okinawa for only one year, I moved the TSD to the Philippines. Clark AB was on the main island of Luzon, and was located approximately fifty miles north of Manila, in the Pampanga Providence. The OSI District 42 Office at the time was located near the center of Clark AB, and was across from the Base Finance Office. The building that housed the OSI Office was a long, one-story wooden building with a central hallway and offices located on both sides of the main hallway. On the far north end of the building there was a large open room that housed the office area for the special investigators. At the time I arrived on Clark, there was a concrete block building, with no windows, located immediately behind the Main OSI Building. At one time, that building was going to be utilized as a communications building to support the District Office; however, that decision had been changed for some reason. So,

Colonel Bill Mears, the OSI District 42 Commander at the time, provided that building for the TSD Office. I coordinated by telephone with Capt. Dwight Caborie, who I had known previously at OSI District 4, and who had been designated as the new TSD Chief. With his agreement, I went to the Base Supply Furniture Section and picked out the desks; cabinets and workbenches I thought would be needed to set-up a TSD Office. I was also lucky enough to know the third person who would make up the new technical team in the Philippines. He was Lenny Boyd, who I had met at OSI Headquarters, when I went through the Basis OSI School. Therefore, the new technical team would start with the advantage of already knowing each other, and a solid basis for a good team.

Shortly after I arrived at Clark, we had what I thought was a terrible Typhoon hit the area. It rained harder than I ever remembered seeing in my life, and the winds were very high. I was complaining to one of the regular agents about how bad the weather was and he told me that what I was seeing was nothing at all compared to the Typhoon and Monsoon weather that Clark had in July of 1972. It had rained a torrential downpour almost all day - - for thirty-two straight days! Everyone was extremely upset with the bad weather and was irritable with each other. Someone made the statement "I thought HE said HE wouldn't flood the world again!"

Another fantastic event that had occurred prior to my arrival at Clark happened in February of 1973. That was when the first group of captives, called "returnees" came back from Vietnam. It had been an extremely joyous occasion, and almost the entire base had been at the Main Air Terminal to greet them. I was told that there had been a lot of preparation for the returnee's arrival. The hospital had been made ready for them and special "soft" food diets had been arranged. This was because it was expected they would not be able to eat much solid food for a while after their arrival, since it was unknown what they had been fed and how much. The returnees changed all of that diet stuff as soon as they got to the hospital. When asked what they wanted to eat - - most of them stated hamburgers, hot dogs and soda! There was much jubilation on the base for the entire time the returnees were there. The children of the base military and civilian personnel had drawn and painted many pictures that were hung in the base hospital.

After I had gotten the new TSD facility completed and the equipment all situated, I had a little time to relax before the other two new personnel would arrive. Therefore, I managed to play a few days of golf at the very nice golf course on Clark. Although the course was flat, it was long and so still presented a challenge. One of the real challenging features out on the course that we had to contend with was you never knew what you might find out there – besides caddies and other golfers! On at least one occasion, I killed a medium sized Cobra Snake on the course. I heard from other golfers that was not an uncommon occurrence.

In late July, Capt. Caborie and Lenny Boyd both arrived at Clark with their families. The first to arrive was Capt. Caborie and his family: wife Josie, Son Tom, Daughter Lorrie and Son Ike. I met them at the Air Terminal on base.

"Hello Capt. Caborie, how was the long flight over?" I asked.

"Please Jake, we aren't at OSI District 4 any longer, you may call me Dwight as long as we aren't in the presence of a higher officer. After all,

we will be working together every day, and we just don't need the formality of rank."

"Thanks – ah – Dwight. That does sound a little strange after the formality Col. Point required back in Maryland."

"Hello Josie, I hope that you're alright after that boring flight. Are the kids doing ok?" I asked.

"Hello Jake, yes the kids and I are fine, just tired of sitting for so many hours."

"Well, we'll get you through customs, and cleared into the main terminal quickly. Being OSI here in the Philippines does have a few advantages. Once you are in the main terminal you can go outside if you want to and walk around. That ought to help."

"Great Jake, that would be so nice. How've you been, and do you like it here?" asked Dwight.

"Well the move down from Okinawa and getting set up here was somewhat of a hassle, but now things are going pretty smooth. Col. Mears has been chomping at the bit to get you and Lenny here and settled down so we can start tackling some of the cases he needs technical support with."

"Yes, I'm sure that's a fact, especially since he used to be the Technical Services Director at Headquarters before Col. O'Leary. I have spoken to him by telephone a few times, and knew he wanted us to get busy as quickly as possible. Do you know of any specific cases he has in mind for us to work?"

"Oh, there are several to hear him talk. I know he will be anxious to talk to you about some of them. In fact, I told him this morning that as soon as I could get you and your family into the Temporary Officers Quarters, I would take you to the District Office for a quick chat, if that is ok with you. Have you heard when Lenny will be arriving here?"

"I expected that Col. Mears would want to see me asap, so I told Josie I'd have to go by the office after we got settled into temporary quarters. I spoke to Lenny three days ago, and he told me he and his family would be traveling to the Philippines next week. Therefore, I am guessing that in a couple more weeks or so, we should be ready to get to work. Have you got the office all set up and the equipment ready to go?"

"You bet Dwight, all we need is a case to start working on. Col. Mears has been out to our office building almost every day asking me if we needed anything else to set up our work space and helping me arrange everything."

"He's really been a great help getting us all of the office furniture we needed."

"That's really great Jake. Thanks for all of the effort you've put in getting the equipment moved down here from Okinawa and getting us an office established."

"It was my pleasure Dwight, it was actually nice to be busy."

The following week, Lenny Boyd, his wife Minnie and son Stephen arrived at Clark. I again met them at the Air Terminal.

"Hello Lenny, it's great to see you again."

"Yes Jake, it's been awhile since we last saw each other at Headquarters. Jake Douglas, this is my wife Minnie and my son Stephen."

"Ma'am, it's nice to meet you. Stephen, how do you do."

"Please Jake, you can call me Minnie."

"OK then Minnie, how was your long journey? Do you have your walking legs back yet?"

"Just a little bit, I really need to walk around soon if possible."

"Yes, I'll get you all through customs and cleared into the main terminal quickly and then you can walk around some while Lenny and I wait for your luggage."

"Great, thanks a whole bunch."

"So Jake, did Dwight make it here alright with his family, and did you get them settled into a place yet?"

"Yes, they arrived just fine, but like you all they were a little worse for wear after that long flight. I put them up in temporary quarters, like we'll do for you guys, and they were able to find a house off base within a few days."

"Yes, I was told we wouldn't get on base housing for a while here due to the housing shortage, so we'll have to live off base until then. Do you have any place you would recommend?"

"I'm hoping to help you find a place near Dwight and Josie if possible. The housing situation off base isn't much better than on base, but not for the same reason."

"Why's that?" Lenny asked.

"Well the crime rate off base is pretty bad in most places, so the Americans normally have to live in guarded communities. Even then, your house will typically have a six to eight foot high concrete block fence around it topped with broken glass."

"Great, I know that Minnie isn't going to like that."

"Yeah, I'm sure," I said, "but it's the best you can hope for here. The Philippines is a great place to be, in a lot of ways, but you just have to get used to the idea these people just don't have much of a life and they envy all we have."

"OK, we'll learn to live with it I'm sure. What about our office and the potential work load? Are we just about set up and ready to start running some good cases?"

"We've got a great office. It is located just outside the back door to the District Office, so we do not have to put up with the BS that goes on in there and they have to ring a bell to enter our building, so we have total control more or less. And as for workload, Col. Mears has been "chomping at the bit" for us to get our act together and get started working technical support cases."

"How is the Colonel? I have not seen or heard from him since he left Headquarters. Has he been in your hair already since you've been here?"

"You could say that," I replied.

CHAPTER 2

I had arranged to be the sponsor for both Dwight and Lenny and had everything arranged to get them settled down as quickly as possible. That was always a chore at Clark. I had taken them around to the limited, desirable housing that was available off base, and they had been able to locate a house that was suitable. Due to the high crime rate in Angeles City, Philippines which was the city located immediately outside of Clark AB, all of the houses that were worth living in, were in fact mini compounds. That was simply an effort to keep the "Stleally-boys" away from the houses. The best security for houses was simply a big, vicious dog, which most military families resorted to as soon as possible. Within a couple of months, all of us were assigned on base housing and the families felt at least somewhat more secure. Clark was essentially a city all its own that was deposited in the middle of a huge fertile plain and surrounded by a sea of people who wanted anything and everything they could get from that city. It was often said Clark was extremely busy during the day but it literally "crawled" with activity at night, most of that activity being illegal!

In fact, the crime on Clark Air Base was so bad; the OSI District Office 42 on Clark was the only OSI District Office in the world that had a fully staffed and operational Night Operations Branch. Their motto was "Nocturnal Vigilance", and on any given night, they were kept very busy.

About a couple of weeks after Dwight, Lenny and I all got situated in our new office, Dwight was called into Col. Mears office one morning to discuss a possible case our technical skills and equipment might be able to be utilized on.

"Yes Col. Mears, what is it we could assist you with?" asked Dwight.

"Well Dwight, I've been approached by the official who runs the U.S. Post Office here on base. There has been a long history of theft of U.S. Government Pay Checks from the mail service here at Clark. There have been multiple attempts by the officials in the post office as well as our own Criminal Investigators to locate how the checks are being stolen or diverted. We are talking about thousands of dollars every month in lost or stolen checks. We have had sources watching the mailboxes, from the exterior of the post office work area to see if they could detect anyone getting into multiple post office boxes to no avail. The Postal Officials have made multiple attempts to detect any of the post office workers who may be stealing and/or diverting pay checks, again to no avail."

"Are all of the postal workers U.S. personnel?" Dwight asked.

"No and of course that's the suspected problem. It is very easy for anyone to cash U.S. Government Checks off base, especially in Angeles City.

Many places will cash Government checks for say fifty cents on the dollar, then turn around, and deposit those checks in a Philippine Bank at face value. There is a lot of money to be made that way. We are probably supporting the communist terrorists off base with this one type of criminal activity."

"Have we made any progress at all in detecting just how the checks are being taken?" Dwight asked.

"No not really; however, recently through extensive sourcing programs, and of course lots of money, we've been able to determine there is at least one of the Philippine workers who is suspected of somehow manipulating the handling of those checks and secreting the checks on his person when he departs for the day."

"What do you have in mind for us to do, sir?"

"Well, I'm hoping that you and your guys can come up with a way of getting some video cameras installed in the post office to watch this particular person or persons. The problem of course is due to the unknown number of people involved in the operation and the nature and the type of internal threats normally involved with the Philippine workers, we can only work with the top Postal Service Official and all installation of technical equipment would have to be done by stealth at night. No one other than the one Postal Official and us must know anything about the operation. Not even the Base Security Police will be given access to any information about this case, so once you enter the building at night, with a key supplied by the top Postal Official, you will be entirely on your own."

"I understand, sir. I will speak to my team and see if we can come up with any possible method to get the job done. Can we arrange to get into the building at night, in the next couple of days so we can see what we can establish as a plan?"

"Yes, I'll talk to the Postal Official, and let you know a date and time."

"Thank you, sir; I'm sure we will be able to complete this technical support for you ASAP."

When Dwight came out to the technical office after his meeting with Col. Mears, he told us what we were requested to do. This case didn't seem too bad at first, but Lenny and I were to learn fairly soon that it was a real problem letting Dwight talk to the Col. by himself as it usually meant we got volunteered to do the impossible, with minimal equipment available, in an excessively short period of time! Dwight just could not say no to the Colonel for any request. Another thing that we soon learned was, after a case was completed and we wrote the technical report for Dwight to sign we got used to the fact we might as well take Dwight a "red pencil" - with the report, as he must have felt he didn't do his job, if he didn't at least make some corrections to the report!

So, two days later in the dark of night, when all postal service employees would have long ago gone home Dwight, Lenny and I were met at the Base Post Office by Major Bud Thomas, the APO Officer in Charge. Thomas let us into the building, and escorted us around to the rear area where the mail was serviced. The entry into the "bowels" of the post office was an education for all of us. The place was a maze of tables, desks and workstations that were nothing more than a table with a large vertical box made up of many pigeonhole slots.

Major Thomas described the typical workday in the post office and how the mail was brought in, sorted and put into the proper mailboxes for the recipients. The workday started for the mail sorters at 7:00 am, as the mail needed to be up in the mailboxes by 11:00 am each day.

Clark Air Base Main Post Office circa 1974 Courtesy of U.S. Air Force

"The mail actually arrives on base via aircraft in large, specially locked material bags. It is then brought to the post office by truck during the early morning hours and placed inside the building. Once the mail sorters arrive for work at the post office, the bags are emptied onto the large tables, where Postal Service Employees first come in contact with the individual pieces of mail and boxes."

"Next, the mail is sorted into piles, depending upon if it's destined to an individual or a base office. Once that has been accomplished, the mail that is for delivery to individual people is then distributed to various workstations for the Postal Service Employees to sort according to alphabetical names and different post office box sections. It is during this individual sorting process we think someone has the opportunity to manipulate the checks and secret them in some manner. That's just a suspicion on our part, but we think it's a good one."

"Once the mail is sorted alphabetically and by box sections," Thomas said, "the employees actually put the mail into the individual mail boxes and that's the end of the process."

At that point, Dwight said, "OK, thanks for the run down on the process Major Thomas."

"Is there anything else unique about this building we should know?"

"No, I think that's just about everything. The trucks bringing the mail back them up to the dock at the rear of the building and unload."

"What are those stairs over there used for?" I asked.

"Oh yeah, those go up to a small office area a few of our administrative personnel utilize."

"May we take a look up there?" Lenny asked.

"Sure go right ahead."

"Pardon me Major Thomas, but do you have any specific employee, or employees, you suspect to be the person or persons involved in the theft of the checks?" Dwight asked.

"Well, yes I do believe that based upon his actions, and the suspicions of one of my best workers, it might be Mr. Pamujong who's taking the checks."

"Can you please show us where Mr. Pamujong works?" I asked.

"Sure, it's this table right over here in the center of the room."

"I notice this particular work station is kind of isolated from everyone, with the way it's situated." Dwight stated.

"Yes, it is kind of. Mr. Pamujong has worked at this station for several years and as I recall he's the one who moved it into this position as he said it gets better light and is easier for him to see his work here."

"OK Major Thomas, at this point if it's alright, we just need to look around to get a better idea of the layout of the room and the work stations. By the way, do you have a photograph of Mr. Pamujong we can have?" Dwight asked.

"Certainly, I'll just go over to my office in the front section. Call me if you need anything."

"Well, guys we need to take a look around and see if there's any place where it would be possible to secret a couple of video cameras. You know it has to be some place capable of hiding those long Sony cameras, so see what you can find. We also will need a place to use as an OP to have the video recorders and the operators. I'll go ask Major Thomas if there's a spare room we'll be able to use for a few days," said Dwight.

As it turned out, the only way we were going to be able to secret any video cameras in the area was to put them above the false ceiling over and near Mr. Pamujong's work center. We decided we would use one camera with a pinhole lens to view the overall area surrounding Pamujong's work center and one camera with a telephoto lens to look closer at the specific work center table and pigeonhole sorting slots, so we could get a closer view of exactly what the Subject did with the mail he was working on.

We also got a break with an OP, as Major Thomas identified a spare room in a hallway outside of the mailroom work area that was only used as storage for excessive equipment. Since the mailroom sorting personnel had no reason to be in that hallway at any time during the day, it would be convenient for us to enter the room by

6:00 am in the morning. We would need to remain in the room until after 11:00 am each day, while the operation was in progress.

"So Major Thomas, we think we've got a plan that will work to catch your check thief," Dwight stated. "We won't reveal the plan to you, so you won't have to worry about compromising the operation."

"That's probably a good thing. Here's the photo of Pamujong," Thomas replied.

"We'll have to submit our operational plan to our headquarters for approval. Once we get approval, I will stop bye and get a key to the building from you and the code for the alarm system. Of course you'll probably want to change the alarm system code after the operation is over."

"Sure, I'll be required to do that by Postal Service Regulations."

CHAPTER 3

It had already been decided by Dwight, that Lenny would be the lead technical agent for this case, so that meant he had to write the operational plan and submit it to Dwight for review, before it was sent forward to OSI Headquarters for their approval. Since this operation was completely on base at Clark AB and involved only DoD Civilians it was not anticipated the approval would take too long to receive. Headquarters technical personnel would simply coordinate with the Criminal Directorate at OSI Headquarters and a courtesy copy of the operational plan would be discussed with the U.S. Postal Service.

After Lenny wrote the operational plan, the three of us sat down and went over it, to ensure it had covered all aspects of what we proposed to do. The plan called for us to install two Sony AVC 3200 Video Cameras in the ceiling of the post office mail sorting room, where they had good coverage of Mr. Pamujong. The associated cables would be strung above the false ceiling to the storage room we were going to use as our OP. Once in the OP, the cables would be hooked to two Sony AV3650 Video Recorders and video monitors. Two Agents would enter the OP at 6:00 am each morning and remain there until approximately 11:00 am. The door to the OP would be fixed so it could be locked on the inside for operational security. The Agents would have to take their own water, snacks and "relief bottle" into the room each day. The Agents would have radio communication with other OSI agents located discreetly outside of the post office building. It was decided the operation would be set to run for two or three days, around the fifteenth of the month payday. Once we had recorded the Subject actually taking any U.S. Government Pay Checks, the

Agents outside of the building would be alerted. They would follow the Subject to whichever military gate the Subject went to and apprehend him at the gate. It was considered by the Base Legal Department that would be sufficient evidence to prove the Subject's guilt in a court of law.

"Well Dwight and Jake, what'd you think does the plan look alright? Do you think Headquarters will approve it?"

"I don't see why not," I said. "I've had worst operational plans approved previously."

"Yes, but this is our first one as a new team, so I sure don't want Headquarters to question us on it," said Dwight.

"Let's look it over again to make sure there're no holes in it," Lenny said.

We went through the complete operational plan again systematically. It looked good, and Dwight finally was happy with it.

"Alright, go ahead and send it, hopefully we'll get an answer back in a few days. Once we get that Lenny, you can set up a start date with Major Thomas."

Lenny and I understood Dwight's position. This was his first command in OSI and he certainly wanted to look good.

Three days later, we got our approval back from Headquarters. They made one slight change in the plan however. Since the payroll checks normally arrived over a period of two days, they wanted us to try to video the Subject taking the checks more than one time, to insure a better chance of having good solid evidence on him. Based upon what we knew about the arrival of the checks and the Subject's suspected habits, we did not think that would present us any problems.

Unbeknownst to Lenny and me, Dwight had sprained his ankle fairly badly over the weekend after we got the approval for the operation. Not realizing how bad the sprain was, he continued to be on it for the rest of the weekend. By Monday morning, Josie had taken Dwight to the Base Hospital where he was admitted with a case of phlebitis. Therefore, he was in the hospital for five days with his leg elevated and was on several blood thinners. After he got out of the hospital, he was on restricted duty for another week. We had already decided we would wait on starting the post office operation until Dwight was back to work, in case something happened during the running of the operation where we needed to change out personnel.

Lenny had notified Headquarters of the situation, and got the approval period for the post office operation to be moved back a month. We still wanted to run the operation over the fifteenth of the month's payday. Lenny and I continued to handle the day-to-day running of the office, and coordinated with Dwight on anything that came up needing his input or approval.

Finally, on the night of the 12th of September 1973, Lenny, Dwight and I opened the back door of the post office with the key picked up from Major Thomas. Lenny immediately went over and turned off the alarm system, while Dwight and I started getting some of the technical equipment out of our Government vehicle. After the three of us got all of the equipment inside the post office building, we locked the rear door and went into the main mail sorting room. We were able to close the shades on each end of the room, so no lights were available outside the building.

"Where do you want to put the camera with the pinhole lens?" I asked Lenny.

"Well we want to cover all of the Subject's work area and also as much of the general area in the room as possible, so I think it should be put about here."

Lenny had picked out a location in the center of the room and along the side of Subject's work area, where he thought the camera would have a good general view of the room.

"Let's hook up a camera to a video monitor and hold it up there where you want to put it," I said. "That way we'll get a picture, before we install the camera. We don't want to put anymore holes in the false ceiling tiles than we have to."

"That's a good idea; however, with all the holes already in the ceiling tiles I don't think another one or two are going to make any difference," Dwight said.

I put a pinhole lens on one of the video cameras, and hooked the camera to one of the video monitors. Then I stood on one of the tables and held the camera up to where Lenny had indicated he wanted to install the camera. The location turned out to be just the right place to get the best view of the Subject's overall work area, and it was just right to see the back portion of the

room clear to the rear door, which is where the employee's entered the building.

"Good pick for the location Lenny, I said. Was that just luck or have you done enough of these installations to have made a good guess?"

"Don't pick on that poor former headquarters weenie like that," Dwight said.

"He deserves every bit of that harassment and more. Besides having been a headquarters weenie, he's from Alabama and you know the only things that come from Alabama are country bumpkins and red necks."

"You're both full of crap," Lenny said. "One of you is a Yankee and the other is a dumb Okie. I don't know why I let those people at Headquarters talk me into coming over here to work with you two!"

And so started our work relationships and long lasting friendships. We became a great technical team, and were able to complete some very good cases together.

After we decided upon the location for the camera with the pinhole lens, we needed to decide where the other camera with the telephoto lens would go.

This camera was going to show a close-up of Subject's work area, and where he was putting the checks in the pigeonhole slots as he sorted them. It would be best if it was placed somewhere immediately behind him, or slightly off to one side.

Upon looking around behind his work area, I noticed there were a couple of holes already in two of the acoustic ceiling tiles.

"What about using one of those two holes that already there?" I asked Lenny.

"That might just work," he said. "Can you hold the other camera up there so we can get an idea of how it looks?"

"Sure," I said as I climbed up on a table and held the camera approximately where it would be located behind one of the holes. I had already connected the camera to a monitor and we got a good picture of Subject's work area.

"That's not bad," Dwight said. "How about trying the other hole and let's see if it is any better."

"I like that second location better," said Lenny.

We had picked the locations for the two cameras, now we had to get them mounted correctly. The camera with the telephoto lens would not be too much of a problem, since the hole was already there, but it still had to be mounted above the acoustic tile at the proper angle to view what we wanted to see. We had a type of camera mount that allowed the mount itself to sit parallel to the ceiling tile on the bottom and a moveable top piece that was hinged in the front. Therefore, the camera attached to the top piece and could be adjusted at any angle from ninety degrees to almost horizontal. It was just a matter of setting the camera back far enough from the hole, so the lens was not readily seen, and then adjusting the angle so the lens looked where we wanted it to and still got enough of the view we needed.

The camera with the pinhole lens was another story. We had to estimate close to where the lens needed to be and then cut a one quarter of an inch hole to put the pinhole lens through the ceiling tile and right up against the bottom of the hole. Since the lens was only one quarter of an inch wide, it could not be moved back away from the hole as the telephoto lens could. With the pinhole lens right even with the exposed side of the acoustic tile, it was always a possibility that someone could see the glass lens and know there was something there. It was one of the chances we took with this type of installation; however, surprisingly few of these installations were ever compromised.

NOTE: However, later in my career, I was told of a case involving a video surveillance in a large base warehouse, where the technical agents did not have any way of properly concealing a video camera. So, the camera was installed up very high in the building rafters and secreted as well as possible. As the investigation got underway, one day early on, the Subject of the investigation just happened to look up and notice the camera. The agents watching the video monitor observed the Subject looking up towards the camera and then he went out of the camera view. The next thing they saw was the Subject looking directly into the camera. Needless to say – that operation ended at that point!

"Well, how does that pinhole look?" Lenny asked Dwight and me.

"It looks good to me," I said.

"Me too," Dwight replied.

"OK, let's get the cables strung over the top of the false ceiling and into the OP," Lenny stated.

We carefully lifted each of the acoustic tiles and moved the cables towards the front wall, where we would have to cross the load-bearing wall and get the cables down the hall to the OP Room. That process took us about a half an hour. We finally got the cables to the OP and dropped them down from the ceiling into the room.

"Lenny, if you will set the video recorders and monitors up on the table there, I'll hook up the cables so we can see what success we've had at getting the cameras into the correct locations," I said.

Shortly after that, we were all looking at an excellent picture of the Subject's overall work area and out to the rear door. However, the view through the pinhole lens was only about half of a picture frame.

"It looks like the camera mount must have moved when we were pulling the cables," Dwight said.

"You guys stay here and I'll go back out and move the camera. You can tell me when we get the best picture," I said.

With just a little movement of the camera mount, Lenny told me that the camera was just perfect.

"Well guys, I think we've got a good installation," Dwight said. "It's almost two o'clock in the morning we'd better get out of here. Let's take one more look around in the mail sorting room to be sure nothing's out of place,

and we did not leave any acoustic tile chips or pieces lying around anywhere. Lenny, will you close up the OP Room while Jake and I look around in the back?"

"Sure thing Dwight."

Dwight and I went into the mail sorting room and started looking around for anything such as debris and/or ceiling tile pieces, trash, etc. We straightened a couple of tables and work centers and by the time we were through, Lenny had joined us.

CHAPTER 4

As we completed the cleaning and straightening up, Dwight looked over at the stairs that led up to the small administrative room. We had not been up there yet.

"We ought to take a look up there, just to make sure what's there and see if there's anything that might be useful to our operation," Dwight said.

"Alright, you're probably correct," I replied.

All three of us walked up the stairs to look around. There were several desks and a few filing cabinets and that was about it. There was a two foot by two-foot trap door in the ceiling, and I had walked over in that direction. Before, both the other guys could say anything; I jumped up on a desk and pushed the door up to look at what might be there.

"I don't know if you should have done that Jake," Dwight said. "What if that trap door is on a separate alarm system than what we disarmed when we came into the building?"

"I don't think that's logical," I replied. "Anyway, we didn't hear any alarm go off."

We continued to look around in the upstairs room for a few minutes and then decided there was not anything there we could use for the surveillance. As we started to go down the stairs, Dwight happened to look outside of the building through an upper window that was even with where we were standing.

"Crap, I see red lights out there. I think the Security Police are here," he said.

"They must have responded to a silent alarm when you pushed up that trap door in the ceiling Jake. Everyone get as far back in the room as you can, and get under something quick. We will just stay up here and hope they do not come up. If they do, let me do the talking." Dwight said.

We got under desks quickly, and remained as quiet as we could. We had not noticed before, but it was warm in that upper room. In addition, with us now worried about compromising the operation, it suddenly became much hotter. We were all sweating profusely, and trying so hard not to make any noise.

We heard the Security Police enter the building and it sounded like three or four people. They came in slowly and were obviously somewhat concerned over what they might find. At first, all we heard was some low voices. Someone must have gone out to the front portion of the building, as they came back into the mail sorting room and stated the front was clear. At about that time, we heard a voice say, "seek em' out boy". It took a second or two for it to register with us, the police had brought in a Patrol Dog. From where we were hiding, we looked at each other and placed our fingers over our mouths, to indicate silence. For what seemed to be an eternity, we heard the people and the dog downstairs walking around. All of a sudden, we could hear the dog making noise with its paws and nails like it was coming up the stairs. Dwight started to get out from under the desk where he was hiding. However, at that moment, we heard a voice say, "It looks all clear. It must've been a false alarm, let's go." The handler told his dog, "Come on boy, let's go".

Within a minute, they had departed the building and locked it up. Shortly after, we could hear the cars leaving. We continued to remain hidden for several more minutes. When we finally did get out from under the desks, we looked at each other and realized all three of us were wet with perspiration.

"Man, that was just too close for comfort," Lenny said.

"I don't remember having been that nervous for an extremely long time," Dwight said.

"Do you want to see me push up that trap door again?" I asked, to which I got two very stern looks.

We relaxed and sat down in some chairs. Dwight decided we should stay where we were for at least another half hour, just in case any of the police had continued to watch the building. Needless to say, we did not get back to our office and then to our homes until very early in the morning.

We all arrived back at our office much later in the day, somewhat tired and haggard looking. Dwight had a message to call Major Thomas.

"Major Thomas, this is Dwight Caborie, what can I do for you?"

"I had a report today an alarm had gone off in this building early this morning. Do you know anything about that?"

"Yes, and I'll tell you all about it in about an hour. I'll come over to see you if that's alright."

"Yes I'll be here. I'll see you then."

Later Dwight went over to the post office and told Major Thomas what had happened and they both had a good laugh. Dwight assured Thomas everything had gone very well and we would be all ready to start the operation on the morning of the fifteenth. Dwight asked if Thomas was sure no one would be entering the room where our equipment was located and Thomas assured him that he had the only other key besides the one he had given us.

Therefore, on the 14th of September, Lenny sent a message to OSI Headquarters notifying them the installation had been completed in the post office and we would be starting our surveillance operation on the next day.

Of course, we did not tell them about the silent alarm and resulting terror we had been through.

At 5:30 am on the morning of the fifteenth, Lenny and I met at our office. We gathered up several video tapes, one of our communications radios and the ledger we were going to use as the surveillance log. Each of us had some bottled water, a thermos of coffee, some snacks and of course our "relief bottles". At 5:50 am, we arrived at the post office. Lenny got out and took all of the stuff we were taking into the OP and went into the building. I took the car over to an adjacent parking area, and then walked back to the post office. Lenny let me into the building and relocked the door. We both went to the OP Room and after entering, locked the door. After setting things up for the hours to come, we put the new video tapes on the video recorders, set the tape counters to "zero", turned on the recorders and monitors and verified we still had good pictures. Lenny made the entry in the surveillance log and we were ready to go.

I looked at my watch and noticed it was almost 7:00 am.

"I see someone coming into the rear door," I stated as I had been watching the monitor while Lenny was completing the log entry.

"Yes, it's about time for the workers to get here."

I started both video recorders and Lenny made the entry into the log that the recorders were activated. He listed the time as 7:00 am. Within just a few minutes, it appeared all of the mail sorting room personnel were at work and the day had started. Lenny made another log entry, as the Subject had gotten to his workstation and started his day. We noticed most of the mail sorters had gone back to a row of tables located near the rear door and had stated opening some of the mailbags that were deposited there last night. The sorting of those mail bags took approximately an hour, and then the individual mail sorters took loose piles of mail back to their work stations to start sorting the mail to be put into the customer's mail boxes. We observed the mail they had at that point appeared to be all first class mail. We noticed the Subject had returned to his workstation with piles of mail.

"Here we go," I said.

"Maybe, Lenny said. I don't see any government checks in that pile of mail thought."

"Yeah, you're right I don't either"

We watched as the Subject started sorting through the pile of mail that he had brought back from the rear of the room. As he started putting mail into the pigeonholes and getting through the pile, we noticed there was a separate group of mail near the bottom of the stack and that mail was entirely government checks. Apparently, when he had been doing the initial sorting of mail in the rear of the room, he had separated all of the government checks into one stack.

"OK, this is different than one would expect to see," Lenny said.

"Yes, this may be what we're looking for," I stated.

As we watched and recorded Subject's actions, we noticed he was now acting somewhat nervous, looking around cautiously to see if anyone was watching him or even near him. With a rather quick movement, the Subject took part of the stack of government checks that had still been located partially under the rest of the mail, on the top of his table, and placed them in a drawer that was located on the bottom right corner of his workstation. He then continued to sort the remaining pieces of mail that was in front of him to include the checks left in the pile.

"Well, I think we've at least an initial portion of the proof we need to put this guy away," I said.

"It certainly appears that way," said Lenny.

We continued to watch the Subject as he started removing the mail and checks from some of the pigeonholes and went towards the individual mailboxes to place the mail in them. He continued doing this until all of the pigeonholes were empty. At this time, it was approximately 9:00 am. The workers all appeared to be going on a morning break at that time. We noticed the Subject seemed to be lingering at his work center, while the remainder of the workers went to the break room. When all of the other workers were well on their way to their break, the Subject quickly opened a small backpack we had not noticed previously sitting below his work center. As soon as he got the backpack open, he opened the small drawer where he had placed the government checks previously and with a quick fluid motion, placed the checks into the backpack. He then closed the pack and walked to the break room.

"OK, we've got him now for the first time," I said.

"We'll have to see what he does with the backpack next," Lenny said.

Lenny made an entry into the log about the time of the event and what we saw.

When all the mail sorters returned from break, they went back to the tables at the rear of the room and got the remainder of the piles of first class mail that had been separated that morning. Subject returned to his work center and proceeded to sort the stack of mail. It was almost an exact repeat of the morning's efforts. He started sorting the mail and putting it into the pigeonholes. Again, when he was about half way through with the stack, he moved the stack partially aside and again revealed a loose stack of government checks. He again opened the small drawer and placed some of the checks into the drawer. He then continued to sort the mail. When he was through with the stack, he started taking the mail and checks from the pigeonholes and went over to place the mail into the individual mailboxes. Once he was all through placing the mail from the pigeonholes into the mailboxes, he walked over to an adjacent workers workstation. They talked for a few minutes and while the Subject was standing at the other person's table, that person completed the same movements we had seen the Subject do while he was moving the checks from the small drawer to his backpack. We could not see exactly what the other person had done, but it was so similar in action to what the Subject had done we became sure the second person must also be stealing checks.

This time I made an entry into the log as to the time and what we had observed.

"What do we do now Lenny?" I said.

"We certainly have a dilemma, he said. I do not want to use the radio to notify Dwight or the other Agents about this, as I do not think that's very secure. I think I am going to take a chance and leave the room, to go report to Major Thomas what we suspect about the second person. You stay here and continue to watch, in case they do something else."

"OK, but be careful going out there.

In a few minutes, I heard a small knock on the door and I quickly opened it.

"Well, the major feels very strongly that both of the people must be involved in the check stealing, as he doesn't think one person could be taking as many checks as have been reported missing on paydays. He is going to call Dwight and ask him and the handling agent to meet him somewhere in a few minutes to discuss what should be done about this situation. He'll also provide a photograph of the second person to Dwight."

"I haven't seen either one of the people do anything else suspicious and I think it must be lunch time now," I stated.

"Ok, the two pouches with the checks are still there below the work stations, so they haven't done anything with them. My guess is they will not do anything else until time to go home for the day and then they will take the pouches with them. I suspect our agents will intercept them both at whichever perimeter gate they chose to exit the base through. We'll just wait for a decision," Lenny said.

CHAPTER 5

A few minutes later, that decision came in the form of a short, cryptic radio message.

"T-1, T-Lead, will stop two. You stay put."

"T-1, roger," I replied.

"Well that settles it, Lenny said. I think we will have this operation wrapped up in one day. We will continue to record until the workday is over to see if anything else suspicious happens. Then we'll wait to hear from Dwight about what to do."

"Sounds good to me,"

The rest of the day went by very slowly. Neither of the two suspects did anything else that appeared to be out of line. All of the mail sorters worked on third class mail the rest of the day. It was all pretty routine at that point. Sort by "pigeon hole", walk to the boxes and place the mail into them. At around 3:15 pm, all of the mail sorters appeared to be getting ready to close up for the day. All mail that had been in the bags had been put into the boxes. They cleaned up the room and got everything ready for the next day.

"It looks like they're getting ready to leave for the day," I said.

"You know, I don't remember any of us asking Major Thomas exactly what the work day is here, but if they come in at 7:00 am, then 3:30 pm is an eight hour day, with a half hour for lunch. I'd better notify those agents outside," Lenny stated.

"T-1 to all, It appears shop's about to close, be alert. The guys have the goods."

"T- Lead, roger. We're on it. We'll be on them to the edge of the yard."

After about a half hour, we got a call from Dwight, both individuals had been detained at the Main Gate to Clark AB. Both suspects had numerous government checks in their backpacks. They were brought to the OSI office and the Philippine Constabulary was notified of the arrests.

At 5:30 pm, Lenny and I were able to shut down the video equipment, and leave the OP Room and make our way back to our office. We would retrieve our equipment later.

"Well Dwight how'd the two guys react when they were stopped and confronted at the gate?" Lenny asked.

"Actually, unlike most of the bad guys caught here in the Philippines, who always start with: Who, me, sir? Oh no, sir, I didn't do that. These two were caught with the evidence right in their backpacks and they just didn't say anything. They are inside, going through interrogation with our Agents right

now. I don't know yet if they will be tried here on base, as U.S. Federal Employees or if they will just be turned over to the Philippine Constabulary. Either way, they're obviously not employed by the post office any longer."

"How many checks did each of them have in those backpacks?" I asked.

"Each one had twenty-five checks. At an average of approximately one thousand dollars per check, that's twenty-five thousand dollars each. I hope that we will find out how long they have been doing this and how many checks they were able to take each payday. And more importantly, where all of the money has been going. It's very possible this thing could go pretty deep into the local economy to include the local government and possibly even further up the chain."

"One thing's for sure, I wouldn't want to be them after our guys finish interrogating them and they're turned over to the Constabulary. No matter who's involved with this whole mess, they probably won't be seen or heard from again," Lenny stated.

"Well, I don't necessarily wish that on anyone, but if you think of the misery those two have caused all of the people whose pay checks they've been taking and the troubles those people must have gone through proving that they didn't receive those checks and then doing without money until

something could be proven that they didn't cash the checks and then claim they were stolen, I guess those two will get what they deserve," I replied.

Dwight stated he was going into the main office and see what else had been learned about the whole thing. He came back a few minutes later and told us the two men had confessed to everything and had told our Agents they'd been taking government checks on and off for over six months. They stated an unknown person who had told them their families would be killed if they did not agree to cooperate recruited them. After they took the checks, they would take them down town in Angeles City the next day and put them into a locked container in a local bank. They never saw anyone take the checks and they would go back to the bank in three days and would find some money in the locked container. They split the money, which usually amounted to about two hundred dollars U.S.

Dwight further stated our Agents, in cooperation with the Philippine Constabulary, had gotten one of the two men to agree to take a few of the checks they'd taken that day to the locked container the next day. The plan was to have the Constabulary watch the container in an effort to catch the person who retrieved the checks. That person would then be utilized to track down where the checks went next. It was a somewhat elaborate scheme at best to be attempted by the Constabulary, but it was the only way to possibly find out who was behind the whole operation.

In addition, there was no way an American could pull off a surveillance like that in Angeles City, as they would certainly stand out immediately. Everyone involved, in the OSI District agreed it was the best way to attempt to resolve the issue, even though, they also all agreed it probably would not work as there were just too many levels of graft outside the gate of Clark AB.

Major Thomas was just happy to get the majority of the government checks back so they could be given to their rightful owners. He was also glad he now knew how the checks were being taken and he could implement new procedures to hopefully keep the thefts from happening again. And of course, he was happy the two men who were responsible for the thefts wouldn't be back in his post office even though it now meant he had to go through the process of hiring two new people and training them.

A few days later, Dwight came back from a meeting in the main office and had the following to report.

"Guys, I just learned from Col. Mears that the Philippine Constabulary informed him today they picked up the person who retrieved the government checks from the locked container in the bank in Angeles City. That person would not cooperate in divulging who else was involved in the operation. It seems that he managed to get loose from his captors and chose to jump in front of a passing truck. In addition, the two post office employees have mysteriously disappeared. So, it doesn't seem like we'll be getting an answer about who was involved in this thing after all."

"Gee Dwight, that certainly surprises all of us I'm sure." I said. "I think I'm beginning to understand how things work here in the Philippines. I'd heard of things like this before, but had never been involved in anything like this."

"I'm sure this won't be the only event like this we'll see while we're stationed here," Lenny stated.

"Well, I guess I'll go in and see what's going on in the main office," Dwight said.

When Dwight returned, he was beaming and advised us that Col. Mears had complemented us highly for completing our first technical operation in such a superb and timely manner. The colonel was extremely impressed.

OPERATION V: THEFT OF CLOTHING ITEMS

Location: Clark Air Base, Philippines
Allegation: Theft of Clothing Items from Base Exchange
Warehouse

CHAPTER 1

As Dwight returned from his latest "stroll" through the main office at OSI District 42 Headquarters, he walked into the technical shop with a grin on his face.

I looked at Lenny with that "Oh No Look" and said, "When're we going to smarten up and not let him go into the front building alone?"

"Yes, you'd think by now we should know better! What've you gotten us into this time Boss?"

"Hey guys, Agent Kline just told me he has a source who told him about a lot of clothing items missing from the Base Exchange. He asked me if we could do anything to assist him with the case. I told him we would need to find out how the items have been reported as missing before we could consider how we might be able to help him. Jake, it's your turn in the barrel. I told Kline you'd be in to talk to him about the case."

"OK Boss, I'm on my way," I said as I glanced at Lenny.

"Hey there Jerry, my Boss says you've got a problem that may need the assistance of the Hobbyshop Boys."

"Oh is that what you 'Prima Donnas' are being called today?"

"Easy there big boy, I know where you live and I can arrange for you to have a visit by the 'Steally Boys' real soon," I replied.

"I thought that was my line," Jerry said.

"Maybe, but I beat you to it this time. What can I do for you this fine Filipino Day?"

"Well," said Jerry, " I've got very reliable information that a lot of clothes items are going out the back door of the BX so to speak. My person says he suspects the items are going missing even before they arrive at the Main BX Building. It seems there are some warehouse buildings the BX uses to store items in when they arrive on base, and before they get brought into the Main BX Building."

"Is there any accountability at all on those items when they arrive in these warehouse buildings?" I asked.

"Yes, my source tells me there are shipping documents that come with the items and those documents then go to the Main BX. Therefore, someone has knowledge of at least what is supposed to be in the BX inventory. Of course, that doesn't always mean much here on Clark."

"Alright then Jerry, can you find out for sure where the warehouses are located, what clothing items appear to be missing, how often they suspect things are going missing, if they have any idea who might be involved in the suspected thefts, and how things might be taken. Based upon those answers, you and I should be able to sit down and come up with a plan of what we may want to do. I'll then need to get OSI Headquarters approval of an operation."

"How long does that usually take?" Jerry asked.

"Normally only a few days, if we've got a good plan," I said.

"OK, I'll get back to you as soon as I can."

Three days later Jerry called and asked if I could come and talk to him about the BX case.

"Hey Jerry, what's up? Did you get some answers?"

"Yes I did Jake, and I think you're going to like them. First, the warehouse involved in this particular situation is located on base, up near the Base Photo Lab. Do you know where that is?"

"Yeah I do, as we use their services a lot."

"Good, second there are several different clothes type items that seem to come up missing on a fairly regular basis, but one of the most popular items to go missing are shoes."

"Shoes? Do Filipinos really want our shoes that much?"

"Apparently they do, because there're many pairs of shoes missing in just the past two months. And third, my source suspects that the Filipino warehouse manager, Mr. Balalong, is being paid a lot of money to provide access to these items. The source literally thinks that these people are so complacent they are operating in broad daylight. He does not have any proof, but he stopped by the warehouse one time during the middle of the morning and found the warehouse manager talking to a suspicious looking character. There was a big American car of some type parked just outside one of the big warehouse sliding doors. When my source asked the manager what was going on, the manager stated the person was his cousin who had just stopped by to visit. The two men looked nervous, and appeared somewhat uneasy as if they had been caught.

"Alright Jerry, you've done your homework, now I'll do mine. I will go up to the Base Photo Lab and look around for somewhere we could possibly setup some video cameras to catch these people. I'll let you know what I find."

The Base Photo Lab was located in the west corner of Clark in a somewhat isolated portion of the base. I had been there several times, but did not remember paying much attention to its construction. As I pulled up to the building, I noticed what I now recalled about it. The entire building was solid concrete. There was a front entry alcove with a formidable metal door, and no windows at all. I made the assumption there must be a rear door somewhere, but I could not see it. I did notice a small wooden slatted shed, which I guessed at approximately six foot square located on the east side of the building. I did not know what was in there, but was relieved it was there because it was on the same side as what I assumed was the long, low BX warehouse building. I got out of my car and went inside.

"Hello, is MSgt. Tyson here?" I asked the person at the front desk.

"Sure, I'll get him," the person replied

"Hello Jake, what brings you out this way?"

"Hey, Sgt. Tyson, would you believe I was out driving around the base and got lost and ended up here?"

"Same ol' line of BS, huh Jake?"

"Actually Joe, can I talk to you in your office, I have a private matter to discuss with you?"

"Sure Jake, come on back."

After we went into his office and he closed the door, he asked, "What's up Jake?"

"I need to tell you first Joe, as always and as a formality, what I am going to discuss is a confidential matter."

"Isn't most of your Hobbyshop Boys stuff that way?" he asked

"Yes, I guess it is at that," I replied.

"Well, this time we've got a source that's telling us some Filipinos are stealing BX items from the warehouse located next door to you on the east side."

"Oh, is that what that building is? I usually see trucks coming and going from there at different times during the day, but never bothered to ask anyone what they were doing."

"Have you ever seen any private automobiles over there?" I asked.

"Now that you mention it, I have seen one or two American cars over there on occasion. Again I didn't question that as it wasn't any of my business," Joe stated.

"Well supposedly that's how the items are being taken," I said, "but we don't know that for sure. I don't see any windows on the side of your building, but I haven't seen the back of this place."

"There aren't any windows at all in this building and only a front and rear door. I understand this building used to be used as some type of high security building that couldn't have windows," Joe said.

"What's the small wood shed on the east side of the building?" I asked.

"That's one of the only utility entries into the building. That is where the compressor for our air conditioning equipment is located. And it's locked."

"Is that someplace I could use to watch the BX Building, if I needed to?" I asked.

"Sure, but it gets a little loud in there any time the compressor kicks in. Needless to say, I'm sure it gets plenty warm in there," Joe said.

"I can't be too picky about some noise. That looks to be the only place in this area where I could possibly watch the BX Building. I consider it lucky it's even there and it belongs to someone who we routinely call upon for confidential assistance. Would it be ok if another agent and I were to set up some equipment in there to conduct a surveillance operation?"

"Knock yourselves out; it certainly won't bother our operation here in the building."

"Do you happen to know if there's a 110vac outlet in there?" I asked.

"I don't know, but I would assume there has to be some electricity in there to run the compressor. Do you want to step out there and take a look?"

"Sure. Is our going out there now, or two people being in there for a couple of days going to present any problems or questions from your people?"

"What time of the day do you think you'll be going in there?" Joe asked.

"We aren't sure just yet. I have to attempt to find out when the transfer of items is suspected to take place. I expect activity to happen by possibly mid-morning. If so, us agents would have to be in place by say 7:00 am."

"That shouldn't present any problem," Joe said, "As we don't open until 8:00 am and I don't have any early birds here except for myself."

"Great, let's go take a look at the shed."

After we got to the shed, I noticed the wooden slats were all installed slopping down, making it difficult to see into the shed. That should make it easy for our video lens to see out between the narrow spaces in the slats. This is due to the lens being focused at a distant view, so it would not see anything up close. When Sgt. Tyson opened the door and we went in, I was a little dismayed. There certainly was not much room in the shed for anything except the compressor. However, there was just enough room on each side of the compressor for someone to stand or sit. I quickly determined there was not an 110vac outlet in the shed, but there was a junction box on the rear wall, which supplied voltage to the compressor.

"Well, I should be able to tap into that junction box and get 110vac," I said. "I may need to get you to shut off the air conditioning system for a few minutes early one morning so I can add that junction box without lighting up like a neon light."

"Shoot, I might not mind seeing that," Joe laughed. "I haven't had a good laugh lately or seen an OSI agent getting fried."

"Thanks Joe, I appreciate your humor!"

"No problem Jake, the place is yours to do with what you need. I have got a spare key inside I can give you. Any idea when you may start your operation?"

"No not yet, but I'll let you know in advance when we are getting ready to go. I will take off now before anyone starts getting to nosey about what we are doing out here. Take care and thanks for your assistance as always."

"Take care Jake, give me a call when you know more."

When I got back to the technical shop, I briefed Dwight and Lenny on what I found. They both agreed the OP location sounded less than desirable, especially in the one hundred degree plus days of summer in the Philippines, but if I was willing to try it, they thought it had a good chance.

"I'll go in and talk to Jerry about what I found out, and see if he wants to work in the OP with me. If he agrees, I'll have him try to get some more information from his source about when another shipment of shoes is due in, and what time of the day the source thinks the thefts might occur."

Jerry was all excited about the possible surveillance and said he did not mind the location. He would get with his source and find out what we needed to know. I told him the shed would be noisy and probably very hot, but it is a perfect location to view the warehouse and maybe get some good video. We would have to enter the shed by about 7:00 am, take plenty of water and snacks with us and of course the ever needed "relief bottles". Everything sounded good to him.

"OK then, I'll complete an operational plan and submit it to HQ OSI for approval. I'll let you know as soon as I get an answer."

CHAPTER 2

The operational plan was relatively straight forward and simple to write. We would install a 110vac outlet in the air conditioner shed located on the east side of the Base Photo Lab. This would provide the necessary power for the video camera, monitor and recorder we would use to monitor and record the activity outside the adjacent BX Warehouse Building. The estimated distance between the shed and the driveway outside of the warehouse was approximately forty yards. We would also need to have a small electric fan to keep the video equipment cool in the expected high temperature we would undoubtedly experience in the shed during the midday to afternoon period. The video camera would be mounted on a tripod. It would view through one of the available slots between the wooden slats of the building. The two OSI agents would enter the shed no later than 7:00 am, and be ready to start the surveillance by 8:00 am. The Agents would take in plenty of water, some snacks and relief bottles. The only person in the area of the photo lab who knew of the operation was the NCIOC of the lab, MSgt Tyson. He was a trusted person, who routinely conducted sensitive support for the OSI District Office. There were no housing areas located near the photo lab and very few other buildings in near proximity.

I submitted the operations plan to HQ OSI on a Wednesday, and had the approval for the plan back the following Monday.

"OK Jerry, we're ready to roll on the BX caper whenever you are."

"Man, you guys do get things done. I have been talking to my source and he is expecting a new shipment of clothes and shoes this Friday. He thinks we should be ready to go on Monday, as he has kept the shipment arrival date to himself. He said if the shipment comes in on Friday, it will not be known to the warehouse people until that day and the warehouse is not open on the weekends. So, Monday would be the earliest the warehouse supervisor would be able to set up a transfer to the bad guys."

"We'll be in place and ready to go early Monday morning. I will go up there in the next day or two and put in the 110vac outlet we will need. After that, it is just a matter of getting there early in the morning, and getting ready to video our friends. I will have Dwight tell the Colonel the status of the operation today. We will need to be here by 6:00 am on Monday to get everything we need and get up to the photo lab. Don't forget water, snacks and a relief bottle."

In the following couple of days, I got the equipment we would use all checked out and ready to go. Since we'd not be able to leave the shed for anything after we got in there, I planned to take an extra video camera and

recorder in case we had any equipment problems. I went up to the Photo Lab and told Sgt. Tyson of our plans and I installed the 100vac outlet box. We were all ready to go.

On Monday morning, I met Jerry at the OSI District Office at 6:00 am. We put all of the equipment into my personal car, as we did not want to use an OSI car, since they might be too well known on base. After we made a second check to be sure we had everything, we were off. I pulled up close to the photo lab on the east side, and we quickly unloaded everything and put it into the shed. At that point, I drove my car about a block away, parked it in the lot of an unused building and walked back to the shed. We quickly got all of the equipment set up and ready to go. It was just past 7:00 am and now it was just sit and wait for the action.

By about 10:00 am it was getting very warm already and we were sweating a lot. We had turned on the fan to attempt to keep the equipment as cool as possible. Nothing had happened yet and we were already getting tired of the heat. All of a sudden, the motor for the air conditioning compressor jumped to life and the noise just about made us both jump through the wooden slats of the shed! I do not ever remember being more startled by anything in my life. After our hearts slowed down again, we regained our composure. We were able to deal with the noise when it came on each time during the day, but it still startled us every time.

By noon, we were baked and had already used up a lot of our water. We ate a lunch and continued to sweat and watch. Somehow, we managed to survive in the heat until about 4:00 pm. At that time, we had watched enough cars leave the Photo Lab to guess most of the personnel had departed for the day. There had not been any activity at the BX warehouse at all. I decided I would take a chance, go around to the Lab, and see if everyone was gone. When I entered the Lab, Sgt. Tyson was in the front.

"Man, you look like death warmed over!" he said.

"I don't know about that death stuff," I said, "but I'm definitely warmed over and over and over" I replied. "Are all of your people gone for the day?"

"Yes, we finished our workload early and I sent them all home. I didn't know if you were still out there or not, but figured if you were you'd certainly want to get out of the heat."

"I owe you several drinks at the Club after this thing is over. Since we can lock the door, I'm just going to leave our equipment in the shed overnight, as we'll be back at it in the morning."

I told Jerry we were through for the day. We walked back to my car and headed over to the NCO Club for a few drinks to cool off before going home. I called Dwight later and told him of what had happened and said we would try again tomorrow. Jerry was going to try to get in touch with his source to find out what happened.

CHAPTER 3

At 6:00 am on Tuesday morning, Jerry and I met again at the office. Jerry said his source told him Mr. Balalong was sick yesterday and had not come in to work. However, he was supposed to be at work today. All we had to do was be sure we had plenty of water, food and new relief bottles, since we had left the equipment in the shed the previous day. We drove up to the Photo Lab, and went through the same procedure as we had the day before. It was about 6:30 am when we both got into the shed and started getting all of the equipment ready. We put on a new video tape, and reset the tape counter on the recorder. We turned on the camera and made sure it was viewing the warehouse correctly. We made the entries in the surveillance log to start a new day.

At approximately 9:00 am, we saw a man park next to the front of the warehouse and enter the building. At 9:30 am, the same man opened a large wooden sliding door on the side of the warehouse facing us. We assumed this was Mr. Balalong.

We immediately started the video camera and recorder, and centered the view of the camera on the open sliding door. Jerry made the entry in the log for the recording start time. For a few minutes, the man was moving boxes around and going through some of them. At 9:45 am, an older green colored Oldsmobile pulled up to the sliding door, from the back of the warehouse, and facing out to the street. A tall Filipino man, dressed in nice American clothes and wearing a straw hat got out of the car and walked into the warehouse. After a couple of minutes, the first man, who we now felt sure to be the warehouse supervisor, and the man who had driven up in the Oldsmobile both exited the building. They stood talking for a couple of minutes.

Jerry said, "This could be what we've been waiting for Jake."

"It certainly looks like it," I replied.

At about that time, the air conditioning compressor motor kicked on again and made such a noise that both of the men we were watching looked over to see what had happened. We remained still and quiet, even though the noise had startled us again as usual. After a couple of minutes, the men dismissed the noise after they figured out what it had been.

As we continued to watch and record, the man from the car opened his driver's door and popped the latch on the car's trunk. To our amazement, right there in broad daylight, the two men started loading what appeared to be shoe boxes into the trunk of the car. They must have put at least twenty-five boxes into the trunk. Next, they threw several shirts and some jeans in on top of the shoes. The man from the car then closed the trunk. He reached into his pants pocket and handed Mr. Balalong something.

"I do believe we just observed the theft of BX clothing items and the payoff to the supervisor." Jerry said.

"I do believe you're correct."

At that point, the second man got back into his car and drove away.

Jerry picked up his portable radio and said into it, "Shed 1 to Chase 1 be advised the dirty bird has flown the coup. Please follow and intercept at the point of departure from the cage, Copy?"

"Chase 1 to Shed 1, copy."

"Shed 1 to Catch 1, please move to the barn and snatch the other bird before he gets away. Be advised the bird may have some chicken feed, Copy?"

"Catch 1 to Shed 1, copy."

CHAPTER 4

Now all Jerry and I could do was wait until the two other Agent Teams had intercepted the Oldsmobile at whatever base gate he choose to exit the base, and Mr. Balalong had been picked up and taken to the OSI District Office. We did not want to exit the shed until after the supervisor had been removed from the building so he would not see us leaving the shed. If all had gone well this morning, we should have video evidence of the theft and payoff and it was only 10:30am. It was just starting to get hot, and we would be out of it in only a few more minutes!

Shortly after the second radio transmission, we saw an OSI vehicle pull up to the BX warehouse. Two Agents exited the car and went into the front door of the building. We had the video tape still running just in case anything else out of the ordinary happened. A couple of minutes later Mr. Balalong, accompanied by the two Agents, closed the large sliding door. Next, all three men exited the front of the building, entered the OSI vehicle and drove away.

At that point, Jerry and I turned off the video equipment. Jerry made the final entries into the log as I started disconnecting the cables from all of the equipment. As soon as we had all of the equipment ready to go, I went to my car and drove it back to the Lab. We packed all of the equipment into my car. I went into the Photo Lab, told Sgt. Tyson we're through, and gave him back his key to the shed. We drove back to the technical shop and Jerry went into the main office as I got Lenny to help me unload the equipment. I informed Dwight about our morning and the three of us started reviewing the video tape. It was beautiful, we had recorded the entire sequence of events and the pictures were just perfect. We quickly made a copy of the tape portion showing the theft sequence on it.

Dwight went into the main office to see what was going on there concerning the case. He came back in a few minutes and said, "Jake, take a video recorder and monitor into the unused interrogation room and get it set up to show the copy of the evidence tape. Then cover the equipment with a sheet, and wait for Jerry to bring in the suspects one at a time."

"Roger that boss, I just love this portion of our job. It's so much fun to see the bad guys faces when they see themselves on TV."

After I had gotten the equipment set up, I notified Jerry everything was ready and went back into the second interrogation room.

A couple of minutes later, Jerry and the supervisor came into the second room. Jerry asked Mr. Balalong, to sit down and started asking him questions again.

"Are you sure you don't know anything about some missing shoes and clothes from the BX warehouse?" Jerry asked.

"Me, sir? Oh no, sir, I don't know anything about that."

"You don't remember a portion of your inventory being reported as missing in the past few months?"

"Oh no, sir, I'm sure I haven't heard anything like that."

"Well, I think that Mr. Douglas has something he'd like to show you."

"Oh, what is that, sir?"

"Just wait, I think that you'll be interested."

I then removed the sheet from the video equipment, and looked at the suspect. He did not register any emotion at that point, as I am sure he did not know exactly what he was looking at.

I then started the video recorder and the first picture to come up was the side of the BX warehouse.

Jerry said, "Do you recognize that place?"

"Oh yes, sir, that's my BX warehouse."

In just a couple of more minutes, the green Oldsmobile came into view and we could see that the suspect was now showing a little more interest.

When the suspect saw the second man exit the car and go into the warehouse, he certainly became noticeably more interested and we could see a small amount of sweat starting to form on his forehead.

"Do you remember this car or this man?" Jerry asked.

"Oh no, sir, I don't believe I've ever seen the car or the man before."

Then, the second man and the suspect came out of the warehouse together and stood talking.

"What about now, do you remember anything now?" Jerry asked.

"Oh, now I remember, sir, that's a man who came by today and asked for directions to the Base Golf Course."

At about that time, the second man opened his car door and popped the latch on the car's trunk.

Next, the second man and Mr. Balalong started loading the shoeboxes into the car. When they were through and had loaded the shirts and jeans, Jerry asked, "I suppose the man was going to take those shoes and clothes over to the Golf Course for the BX?"

"Oh yes, sir, that's what he told me."

The last thing that Mr. Balalong saw on the videotape was the second man reaching into his pants pocket and handing the suspect something.

At that time Jerry said, "And I suppose what the man just handed you wasn't the money we found in your pocket this morning when those two OSI agents picked you up?"

"Oh no, sir, I've had that money for quite some time now. I was planning on having a friend of mine, who works at the BX; buy my wife some cooking pans for her birthday."

"Well, we'll see what the other man has to say when I interview him next," Jerry, said. "Meanwhile, I think the Philippine Constabulary wants to talk to you."

"Oh please, sir, I don't want to talk to the Constabulary. I'll tell you anything you want to know."

"I'm afraid it's a little too late for that."

"Jake, please come back in about a half an hour while I get rid of this guy and have an initial talk with the other man."

"OK, how about just giving me a call when you're ready."

"Sure thing, Jake."

About forty-five minutes later, Jerry called and asked me to come back into the second interrogation room. As I entered the room, Jerry was there with the man from the Oldsmobile.

"Mr. Douglas, will you show Mr. Mubuah your interesting video please?"

"I'd be more than happy to Jerry."

As I removed the sheet and exposed the video recorder and monitor, the suspect became interested. I pushed the play button and sat down to watch the show. As the first scene came on the monitor, it showed the BX warehouse. Next, the Oldsmobile was observed coming into view.

"Do you recognize that place and the car?" Jerry asked.

"On no, sir, I've never seen that place and I don't recognize the car."

The next scene showed Mr. Mubuah getting out of his car and entering the warehouse. A couple of minutes later, both Mr. Mubuah and Mr. Balalong were seen coming out of the warehouse and talking.

"Do you recognize the man in the picture with you?"

"Yes sir, that's Mr. Balalong, he is my neighbor. But that isn't me in the picture"

"That isn't you? It certainly looks just like you to me. Jake, doesn't that look like Mr. Mubuah to you?"

"It looks just like he looked this morning, when I made this video of him at the BX warehouse."

"Do you remember seeing Mr. Balalong today?"

"Oh no, sir, I think that picture must've been taken a couple of weeks ago, when I stopped bye to visit him."

The next scene was when the suspect opened the trunk of his car and then the video showed the two men loading the shoes, shirts and jeans into the trunk.

"Do you recognize that, and isn't that the BX property that was in your car this morning when you were stopped at the gate? I mean, we have your car outside, and we have all of the BX property that we found in the trunk of your car. Don't you think it would be best to just tell us all about this matter?"

"Oh no, sir, I swear to you that is not me. There must be someone else who looks just like me."

"Alright, if that is your story we can end this interview. I will take you back into the first room where we were. Jake, please stay here, I have someone else that would like to see your picture show."

As Jerry took Mr. Mubuah back to the first interrogation room and opened the door, there was Mr. Balalong and two Philippine Constabulary Officers.

"You can wait here for a few minutes please," Jerry said.

When Jerry came back into the room, he had a Philippine Constabulary Officer with him.

"Jake, I'd like you to meet Colonel Papango. He is the local Philippine Constabulary Commander. Would you please show the Colonel your picture show?"

"Sure Jerry, I'd be happy to."

After viewing the entire video two times, Colonel Papango got up to leave the room.

"Well Mr. Jerry, if it's alright with you and your officer, I'll take the two men to our office for further interrogation. I do not think that they will be causing you or the BX anymore troubles in the future. I am sure they will be going to jail for a long time. Thank you Mr. Jake, for your excellent video surveillance and evidence. It's a pleasure to work with the OSI."

I went back out to the tech shop and started cleaning and putting away all of the video equipment. After that, I started writing the Report of Investigation. When I was through, I took the report to Dwight, along with a red pen, for his review.

Then – I sat down and started talking to Lenny, as we began waiting for the next case.

THE AUTHOR

Special Agent Jack Dyer retired from the United States Air Force in October 1980 following nine years as a radio repairman and then eleven years as a technical agent in OSI. He retired as a master sergeant.

He was one of the first Non-Commissioned Officers in OSI Technical Services to have been a Technical Chief, twice.

After retiring from the U.S. Air Force, he worked for fifteen years in the special security arena of the Aerospace Industry in Southern California. Following that, he worked as a special investigator in the Contractor Background Investigations Field for the U.S. Government.

Jack and Michele, his wife of fifty-one years, make their home near Bozeman, Montana. They have three children, five grandchildren and three great grandchildren.

Made in the USA
Charleston, SC
17 August 2014